The  's

of an
Old Codger Named Jim

Part II: N to T

AKA ... Jim Gildersleeve

The ABCs of an Old Codger Named Jim
Part II: N to T

by: James P. Gildersleeve

inspiration & general complicity:
Robin R. Gildersleeve

Design and layout by James P. Gildersleeve
Printed in the United States of America

List of Jim's ABCs

Introduction

This is the continuation of a book begun as, what turned out to be, Part I of *The ABCs of an Old Codger Named Jim*. In that book, I became a little more expansive than I had intended and I stopped with the chapter 'M is for Mackinac'. So, this book, Part II, picks up with 'N is for Nacromancy', and goes through 'T is for Trump'. It seems I've not learned how to regale you within a reasonal number of pages. Part III will be out soon, I hope.

Just to remind you, the focus of these books is on the exciting world of interesting words … and the trivia associated with them? I selected words that appealed to me for reasons unexplainable … I simply thought they would generate tales you might find entertaining. I hoped I would be able to generate interesting facts or stories regarding their meaning or usage.

I have to acknowledge here the importance of another author's works. Sue Grafton, who who had passed away just before I began, is the author of what's been called the 'alphabet series' of detective novels that propelled her into literary prominence. Her success with that series of novels made me stop and think that her device of hitching stories to the letters of the alphabet might be a way to approach this book.

So, I began: *The ABCs of an Old Codger Named Jim* – namely me. Rather than write an entire book centered on each letter of the alphabet, as Sue Grafton did, I've reduced the creative intensity involved by focusing on one letter for each chapter of my book. It's not that I'm lazy, but I just can't envision myself writing 26 books – 26 chapters will be difficult enough.

Now, you might be wondering how I selected the word to explore for each letter of the alphabet … for example, *A is for Aardvark*. Good question. It's simply a result of an exhaustive examination of my imagination – what tickled my interest at the point of time that I began writing each new chapter. Aardvark, for example, was selected because I liked the double-A spelling of the word and I knew very little about them. I thought it would be interesting.

When I started, I had no preconceived idea of what words would be used for each chapter. I chose aardvark, wrote the chapter, and then began consideration of what should follow in the B chapter. Each successive chapter followed a similar path.

I hope you find this collection of stories focused on words I find interesting to be intriguing. If not … well … I'll have another book to gather dust on the shelf above my computer.

James P. Gildersleeve

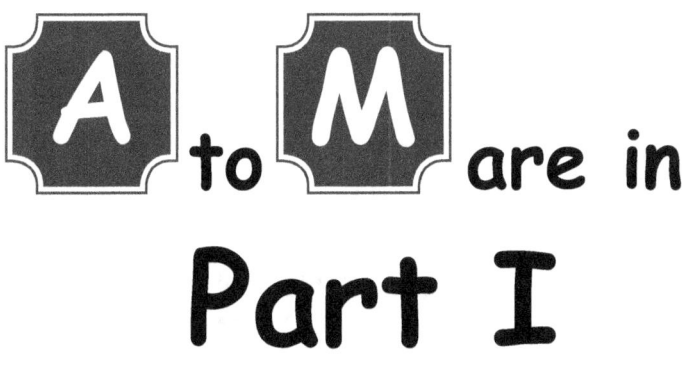

A to M are in
Part I
of 'The ABCs of an Old Codger Named Jim'

The first 13 chapters (A to M) of my 'ABCs' book are in Part I. As you noticed if you read the first book, I obviously became more verbose than I had originally planned.

I have divided this book into three parts in an effort to keep each book more manageable. Of course, that means readers will have to wade through more pages to fully appreciate my take on words selected.

If you're starting your foray into my world with this book, I encourage you to explore the stories in Part I … and in Part III, when its ready. I assure you, they are (will be) equally entertaining (my evaluation) … and equally unusual.

So … now on to the new stuff!

***

N is for Necromancy

Necromancy is hardly a word used in everyday conversation ... in fact, it is mentioned only with hesitation when speaking of the blackest of magic. It's scary in its connotation of evil in all aspects ... of one's ability to converse with the dearly departed living in the nether reaches of hell. What a great word ... what a rich source of material to explore in this chapter.

My first thought was that tales about such a 'haunting' subject might lead me into a realm of ridiculousness ... and it would be difficult to sustain any sense of reader attention. But then I thought of several interesting story lines that could be explored, and my trepidation of entering that realm swiftly dissipated. After all, my 'challenge' in writing this book was to ingeniously overcome such obstacles.

So, what are the 'dead' telling me to write about? Well, there's always the one about a novice playing in a Dungeons & Dragons game who found he had an affinity for necromantic spells … or, a young family-man who was blessed with the ability to converse with the dead.

Ah, yes … it's all coming into focus. The game … as Sherlock was prone to say … is afoot.

***

An Adventure Sure To Please

Arnold sits alone at the Dungeons & Dragons game table ... where three others had sat just moments before. Their sudden disappearance loomed large as he recollected the D&D game underway when his character, Zolis, a Sorcerer, cast a necromantic spell ... made-up to give his character time to achieve the game's goal ahead of his opponents.

The spell casting chant he articulated was conceived on the spur of the moment, and he took pride in its originality and pertinence to the spirit of the game. His words ...

> *"Hocus, pocus ... smashing, thrashing ...*
> *Focus on your quest, with dangers crashing.*
> *Gather 'round our table ... don't be nerds ...*
> *Sit with backs straight, and hear my words.*
> *When this chant ends, and I stifle a yawn...*
> *You will gape wide eyed, and all be gone"*

These words tumbled out ... and Arnold smiled roguishly while trying not to yawn. It was then, as his eyes looked up, when he expected the Dungeon Master to roll the dice and impose the impact of his spell on his competing characters ... that his friends, not the game characters, disappeared. The inexplicable had happened ... he was alone. He stood and looked around. "All right ... where are you guys? Fun's fun, but you can come back now."

But his friends did not reappear. "This can't be happening," he thought to himself. "It's a game ... a silly game."

_____

This was Arnold's first venture into the game of Dungeons & Dragons. It all started that morning when his buddies had insisted he join them in their weekly game at Clark's house. "It'll be a lot of fun," his buddy Clark said. "You will be captivated by an adventure sure to please." He had resisted all previous efforts to get him involved ... he really wasn't into role playing games, no matter the thrill of adventure they promised.

This week, however, one of their foursome couldn't come and they desperately needed Arnold to complete their group, so he agreed. Actually, Arnold had accepted his first venture into the D&D world created by his friends with a bit of curiosity ... and he sensed this wasn't the time to say 'no'.

It was Sunday, and as the foursome sat down at the kitchen table, he was introduced to the campaign and the characters. His friend Clark, the Dungeon Master, sat on his left, and he explained, "We are in a 14th century scenario involving the challenge of finding and vanquishing Count Vlad, the Impaler. During the previous two weeks, we have moved ever closer to catching Count Vlad ... and none of our characters has thus far surrendered their heads to be impaled on a stake along the road to Count Vlad's

Walachian castle.

"Pete and Joey ... and you ... will each be seeking to overcome all obstacles imposed by my scenario to win the game. The challenge is to find and end Count Vlad's reign of terror ... and you each have abilities and weapons to bring to bear in that task."

Clark took Arnold to the side and pulled out a partially completed Character Sheet. "In this adventure, you are a humanoid wanderer ... a survivor ... a Sorcerer. You have both intelligence and wisdom, with high ratings in intimidation and arcana, and your name is Zolis. You are also skilled with cantrips of suggestion and the use of flaming spheres ... and the equipment you carry include darts and a quarterstaff which serves as an arcane focus. But your primary ability is the use of spells ... particularly necromantic spells learned from interactions with the dead. You are a formidable force in our little adventure.

"Pete," who was sitting across from Arnold, "is a Hunter-Warrior and is skilled in the martial arts. He never backs away from any challenge, and he considers the quest to defeat Count Vlad to be his sworn duty to complete.

"Joey," sitting to Arnold's right, "is a Knight of the Templar order, and he's a swordsman who has never been bested. He has a chivalrous nature and a predisposition to help those in need. The victims of Count Vlad weigh heavily on his heart and he has sworn to exact revenge on their behalf.

"Each of you is competing against others to overcome the challenge and be the one who takes down Count Vlad. As the new player, Arnold, you enjoy the benefit of being unpredictable to Joey and Pete … but, you are also at a disadvantage in not knowing their predispositions on the hunt. Are you ready?"

With all the explanations out of the way, the foursome began their play. Each in their turn proceeded to tackle obstacles imposed by the Dungeon Master on their adventure within the limitations of their abilities and the consequences of challenges encountered. There was very little direct contact of the characters with each other early in the afternoon, but as the play continued, the three approached Count Vlad's castle and direct competition seemed assured.

It was then that Arnold had decided that he needed to slow down his friends to give himself the time needed to achieve an advantage. "This is a chance to make use of my unique abilities," he thought to himself, "and deploy a spell that keeps them from reaching Count Vlad before I do. Hmmm." And making them disappear seemed like the way to do that, so he considered the various chants at his disposal and decided that an original spell might be better than those on his Character Sheet.

It was that decision … and the seriousness of his

play … that created the situation he now faced. His chant had caused his friends to disappear, and he felt responsible for whatever had happened to them. But he realized it wasn't Zolis that caused this … it was Arnold himself. And it was Arnold who would have to find his friends and bring them back.

As he mulled over his options, it suddenly turned dark, and the table at which he sat seemed to be floating in a void … devoid of any surrounding features of Clark's kitchen. He found himself sitting there with a group of 10 or so 'animated corpses' in various stages of decomposition. They appeared soulless and gruesome to look at, and they looked at Arnold with a 'hunger' in their eyes that terrified him. They all seemed curious as to how they had come here … and why.

Arnold thought back to Clark's explanation of his character's proficiencies and remembered that Zolis had an ability in necromancy which is based on being able to communicate with the dead. Relying on a bit of his Zolis character, he braced himself and put up a brave front. He asked, "What brought you here? Where are my friends?"

His visitors huddled around the opposite side of the table glaring at him, mumbling and twisting without moving closer. Although they didn't speak, Arnold understood them to say, "We have not come to you. It is you who has come into our realm. Your search for others is not our concern."

Arnold responded, "But you must have some idea on where ....."

He was interrupted with a sudden thought coming from his newfound friends, "Consider the manner in which they were lost. One can only find something lost by following the path they trod at the time of the losing."

Arnold thought back to the D&D game in play at the time his friends disappeared. He had conjured up a chant that elicited a reaction, and that reaction was to have his friends 'be gone'. Perhaps, he might find them by invoking another spell as Zolis that would enable him to rejoin his friends. With that realization, the visitors at his table faded away with a parting thought, "Take heart ... your time in this void is short lived. You are not yet one of us, nor are your friends. Adieu ... and be hasty ... time in the void can be haunting."

"OK," Arnold thought, "What spell can I cast that will end this nightmare?" His objective was to rejoin his friends, so ... he closed his eyes, evoked Zolis and said these words with all the conviction he could muster:

> *"Hocus, pocus ... fidgety fast ...*
> *I beseech ye soulless shadows ... now long past.*
> *Show me the way, this ordeal to end ...*
> *Give me the ability, my friends to defend.*
> *Let us reunite, and find our way ...*
> *Back to our innocent game ... straight-a-way!"*

As Arnold concluded this chant and opened his eyes, he found himself in a twilight zone of emptiness, with nothing of substance to his left or right … straight ahead or behind … just a nothingness that was severely disturbing. He could not tell whether it was daytime or nighttime … nor if he was awake or dreaming. But, he suddenly realized that his friends were materializing in the void with him, and they looked as startled at his arrival as he was in his arriving.

With obvious relief and a newfound sense of optimism, they quickly moved together and enjoyed a group hug that reflected their long-time friendship. Clark was the first to speak, "What happened to you … and how did you get here? Do you know how to get home?" The others quickly chimed in, and Arnold found himself at the center of their hope for rescue from this unexplainable emptiness.

"I'm not sure," he responded to virtually every question being thrown at him. "It seems that my game character … Zolis … has tapped into a netherworld … sort of an underworld of dead souls that he commands and who respond to the spells he invokes. When my chant during our D&D adventure game suggested that 'all be gone', you were literally whisked away … disappearing from our game table. I found you here by creating another chant seeking our reunion.

"My hope," he continued, "is that we might all

return to reality by having my alter ego, Zolis, invoke a new chant that communicates to the dead our desire to find the road home." Although they all looked skeptical, no one had a better idea for resolving their predicament. Discussions then focused on what words to include that would allow them to get back to the safety of Clark's kitchen table.

Just then, they heard an increasingly loud roar from the distant reaches of their emptiness. As the clamor grew louder, a thundering herd of beasts charging in their direction came onto view. These were not like any animals they'd seen before. They were three legged creatures with two long horns atop what appeared to be a head. Beneath the horns was a series of five eyes and a gaping mouth filled with teeth snapping and grinding together … not your conventional herd of domesticated bovines. And they looked hungry.

Arnold and his friends looked around to find refuge. Finding none, Joey said, "Arnold, I think you'd better spin that spell to get us out of here! Let's just hope it works … quickly!"

Arnold thought of the words they had discussed and closed his eyes as he … and Zolis … started this chant:

"Hocus, pocus … hippity hop …
Beasts are coming, running non-stop.
They're ugly and they stink, hungry too …
I fear we're fodder … for a beastly stew.
Take us to safety … no more to roam …
Give us another day, in our worldly home."

As the stampeding beasts moved ever closer, Arnold and his friends banded closer together … eyes darting around … still looking for someplace they might find safety. Joey fearfully asked, "When is your spell going to save us … your pals from the netherworld need to step on it or we're goners."

Arnold nervously shrugged and admitted he didn't know. "I'm new to this. I don't know how or when they will respond to the spells I chant."

Just as the beasts were upon them, the foursome as a group suddenly levitated above the herd. Looking this way and that, the beasts appeared mystified at having lost Arnold and his friends. But seeing them floating just above their heads, they thrust their horns high … reaching futilely for their prey who had now risen out of reach. Then they thundered off … and just as the beasts had appeared out of nothingness on the far horizon, they suddenly faded into obscurity on the opposite side.

Pete exclaimed, "Wow. That was close. Please explain how you did that, Arnold. How did you come by this mystical ability to manipulate our environment … and our movements in this void?"

Before Arnold had a chance to answer Pete, they all suddenly fell to the ground … each feeling the discomfort of a hard landing … but the savage beasts were no longer in sight. Looking around, they saw that they had landed in a clearing with gnarled, mangled trees and an impenetrable thicket all around … with long, savagely bent branches enticing Arnold and his friends into their grasp. It was twilight and the darkness just compounded the eeriness of their surroundings.

A path invitingly appeared on their left. Not seeing any other way through the thicket closing in around where they lay, they unanimously agreed to head in that direction. They quickly rose on shaky legs and ambled toward the opening, staying clear of the beckoning tree limbs that seemed to stretch out in their direction as they passed.

While they didn't know what lay down the path, they walked with a growing sense of optimism that home was just ahead. After all, they had escaped the 'void' and the raging beasts … they had 'flown' out of danger and avoided being impaled when they landed in this ghostly forest … and they were all together. But, they hadn't gone far when the bounce in their step turned to a cautious plodding as the path to salvation took an eerie turn.

"Did you hear that," said Clark. "There's something coming from behind us." They stopped and listened … what initially was a faint murmuring was clearly getting louder … and closer.

"It sounds like a mob of … dare I say … 'zombies' grunting and groaning … just like the soulless creatures I met before," Arnold responded, "but these guys don't sound friendly … nor do I think they bode well for our journey. We've got to get off this path and hide … quickly!"

The four friends scampered to the side of the path seeking an opening in the thicket where they might hide. Clark suddenly called out, "Here's a pocket beneath the shrubbery that may work … it's small, but I think we can get in." One by one, they all followed Clark into the hollow … pulling a limb behind them to hide their route.

Arnold looked around at their lair and commented, "This looks like it might be the home of some animal out scrounging for his supper. I hope whatever it is that lives here doesn't return while we're here and think that dinner has been delivered!" They all looked around cautiously, and a dread descended over them.

What they saw at the rear of their hiding spot was an area of webs lining the brush and extending back into the interior … and lodged in the webs were globs of substances looking an awfully like spider egg sacs … but much bigger than usual. Clark … who was the furthest back in their hiding place … and closest to the webs … said with obvious fear in his voice, "What have we gotten ourselves into? We may have temporarily escaped whatever is out there, but are we in even greater danger in here?"

Arnold ... looking back from whence they came ... said in an almost whisper, "Shhh. We have a more pressing danger." The mob of creatures was now passing where they were hiding ... and they sounded irritated. Peeking through the gnarled branches hiding their location, he whispered, "One of our friends out there has stopped ... he's looking suspiciously in our direction and appears to be sniffing for our scent. Don't move!"

All movement stopped as they waited for this latest danger to pass ... but, the curious one inched closer. Arnold thought to himself, "What are we to do if this creature finds us?" Options were not good! "Can I invoke another spell that will dissuade it from uncovering our hiding spot?

"Wait," he suddenly thought. "What had Clark said about my character's abilities? Not only was Zolis skilled in the use of necromantic spells, but he also had abilities in the 'power of suggestion and the use of flaming spheres'. Can I maybe 'suggest' to our friend out there that he should turn away?"

Without taking the time to tell his friends, he closed his eyes, reached down into the depths of his being and suggested under his breath in the strongest possible terms:

"Clickity clack ... clickity clack ...
Give my friends and me some slack.
You've taken the wrong tack ...
And it's time you get back on track.
Rejoin your friends on the path at your back ...
Clickity clack ... clickity clack!"

After repeating this ditty three times, Arnold saw
the creature turn and move on with the marauding
group away from their hiding spot. His 'suggestion'
had worked. Just as soon as they disappeared from
view, the four friends scampered out of their refuge,
glad to be away from the webs and spider sacs ... but
still worried about the absent owner of their hideout.
They all shuddered thinking of the predicament they
had been in.

"Come on," said Clark. "Let's get out of here. We
need to follow our path ... hopefully back to the
table in my kitchen." With that, they all quickly
moved in the direction they had been traveling ...
away from the 'void' and their web-filled refuge in
the thicket.

After a time, they found themselves more optimistic
about their situation. But, danger continued to lurk
around every turn in the road, and it was around one
of these bends that they encountered a new threat.
Up ahead, the path was crowded with hundreds of
large spiders ... tarantulas ... that were moving in
their direction ... possibly to the lair they had just
vacated.

"This doesn't seem to be anything a Zolis' spell or suggestion will resolve," offered Arnold. "I wonder if one his 'flaming spheres' will help?"

Again, he reached down into his character and began whirling his hands in a circular motion. As he rotated his hands, a ball of fire appeared between them and grew larger and brighter the longer he played with it. Strangely, his hands were not affected by the fire. When it had grown into the size of basketball, he reared back and swung the flaming orb at the onrushing spiders … and they in turn burst into flames. He repeated this several times till the spider threat became nothing but a scattering band of blazing critters … no longer threatening.

They smiled as they continued along the path. The spiders … now clumps of smoldering ash … were quickly put behind them, and it appeared the road ahead was brighter. Before they knew it, they emerged from the ghostly forest into bright sunlight, and there ahead of them was Clark's house.

Without a word, they entered and sat down around the kitchen table … as if they had never left. Silence continued for a time as they thought back on the adventure just completed … a far cry from the D&D game normally played at this table. Each of them frequently glanced around … nervously hoping Clark's kitchen would still be there.

"Arnold … I'm not so sure we'll want you to fill in again for our little game," commented Clark with a chuckle. "Your participation seemed to raise the level of excitement, and I don't think we're up to traveling that road again."

"Ditto," responded Arnold. "This has not been much fun for me either. While I was 'captivated' … encountering hoards of soulless creatures, being nearly trampled by stampeding beasts, battling a swarm of giant tarantulas, and being scared out of my wits throughout the entire ordeal … it was not my idea of 'an adventure sure to please'."

Silence again descended on the table. No one seemed to want to put into words all that they had experienced. After a while, Joey asked, "What do we tell our friends about this afternoon?"

Clark replied, "Nothing! No one would believe us anyway. Would you?"

***

Spooky Memories

My first encounter with a 'Spooky' ... that's what I call my visitors from beyond the grave ... happened when I was sitting on a park bench in San Antonio, Texas. It was a sunny day in May and it couldn't have been nicer. In a city known for its hot and humid climate, I should have been enjoying my alone time. But, this was not a happy time for me.

I had just received an emphatic "no way" response from Linda, the girl I thought I was going to marry, to join me for a dinner date. Obviously she was not as serious about our 'relationship' as I was. Of course, we had only gone out on one date, but I knew she was the one. Her decline ... the seventh in a row ... was devastating.

It was in the depths of my doldrums that a Spooky appeared sitting beside me, slowly coming into view as if from a mist. I was so far into my grief over having been turned down ... again ... by Linda that this apparition didn't even phase me. Nor did his dress, which appeared to be from the mid 1300's in a rather disheveled condition. And his demeanor was clearly more exuberant than mine.

When he had materialized fully, he rose and faced me as I remained seated ... by now somewhat dumbfounded. He doffed his fancy velvet hat with a plume and greeted me with a flair. "Good day, young man. You are strangely garbed. Wherefore art thou from?" He was clearly not Texas born! He was wearing a snug-fitting jacket of hip length and loose fitting trousers, over which he wore a multicolored tunic.

I looked around as others in the park strolled by and cheerfully cavorted on this beautiful day nearby. They seemed oblivious to this strange man standing in my presence. Why wasn't he an instant curiosity? Why didn't anyone but me think his sudden appearance was strange?

By now, I was beginning to get a little nervous … who was this guy … and where did he come from? I felt I should respond, but couldn't bring myself to acknowledge what was clearly a figment of my imagination … or was it?

"My name is Charles … and I'm a Texan by birth," I finally said.

My imaginary friend responded, "How do you do. My name is Romeo Montague, and I'm from Verona, a village in the Northern reaches of Italia. I'm here to give you advice on matters of the heart … not that my experience has been very successful. I have been fortunate to have loved … and lost … a soulmate of extraordinary beauty and elegance … a romantic like me. You, my friend, are a novice in such matters and have much to learn."

With that, he proceeded to offer his thoughts on the

art of 'wooing a fair maiden', as he put it. "Does her dwelling happen to have a balcony?" he asked. "I'm great with courting my love on a balcony. But, in all seriousness, the traits most admired by young ladies are sincerity and a sense of humor."

I sat back on that park bench and listened raptly to Romeo's suggestions. He continued his discourse on how to 'romance' my lady-love while pacing in front of my bench for quite some time … answering all my questions with exaggerated theatrics that would have greatly pleased Shakespeare. Figment of my imagination or not, his advice was intriguing … and welcome. Might I have better success with Linda by adopting Romeo's old fashioned ideas? I gradually thought that such might be the case.

Following his lengthy critique on wooing, Romeo suddenly stopped his pacing and declared, "That, my friend, is the extent of my advice. Follow my ideas and this young lady of yours will respond favorably and be your best friend and lover for all eternity."

With that being said, he smiled broadly, doffed his hat once again, and faded into just a memory. Still, those strolling past seemed not to have noticed this unusual event ... a strangely garbed man in their midst … and his sudden disappearance.

While I still question my sanity as a result of that initial experience, visits by other Spooky's after that have made me a believer … I am gifted in necromancy … the ability to converse with the dead.

Now, does that sound insane, or what?

On the bright side, 13 years after my visit with Romeo, Linda is now my wife and we have three children. I guess you might say his advice paid off ... I'm now more of a romantic than I thought I ever could be, and happier than I have any right to be.

I did not have another encounter with a Spooky until Linda and I were in the third year of marriage. I was very happy in my job as a marketing specialist in the WalMart corporate offices and we had just gotten settled in our new home in Bentonville, Arkansas. Everything was going well when suddenly our first born daughter, Sara, became seriously ill.

Sara had an infection which progressed from a simple cold to a serious bout of pneumonia ... we hovered over her bed as she struggled with her breathing and a hacking cough that were taking their toll on her ability to fight back. The doctor prescribed antibiotics and offered encouragement as best as he could.

As the seriousness of Sara's condition increased, she was admitted to the hospital where the full resources of modern medicine could be applied. However, our two-year old blessing grew weaker as we watched ... and our worries increased knowing there was little more we could do to help.

Two days after Sara was admitted, I was becoming as worried about Linda as I was of Sara ... Linda was exhausted from her constant vigilance and her attention to Sara's needs. I finally convinced her to take a break and nap for a time in the bedroom provided for families, assuring her I would remain at Sara's bedside.

It was while I sat alone with Sara, head bowed in prayer while she slept, that I suddenly realized a presence was standing over her … smiling broadly. He was dressed in what looked like a tunic of tan sackcloth that stretched to his knees and was secured with a belt of rolled cloth around his waist. He wore sandals and had a brown outer robe with short sleeves that covered the inner tunic and draped open in front. Not your typical medical staffer.

He looked up and turned in my direction … gazing at me with hypnotic eyes … and said, "My name is John … some call me John the Baptist. I understand you have doubts about the mercy God can bestow on his children and the power of prayer. I bring you a message from our Maker … 'fear not, for all is possible if you believe in our Lord'. Do you believe?"

Having previously rationalized my meeting with Romeo as being the result of some necromantic skill I possessed, the sudden appearance of John the Baptist didn't seem so odd. Especially since I had just then been severely despondent and desperately praying for a miracle that would help Sara get through her illness. I wanted to believe, both in the idea that John the Baptist was actually here in response to my prayer, and that all things were possible through faith in Him.

I responded, somewhat dejectedly, "What I believe is that Sara is precious to me and that her loss would be tragic and unbearable. I want to believe in God's mercy. But, I'm afraid when I pray for His help, I plead for a miracle that I consider may be beyond reach rather than having faith in the certainty of His mercy."

John moved closer to me, and said, "I'm here to allay your uncertainty. You must have faith … as He said 'all things are possible' but you must believe with deep conviction that God has a plan for Sara. Whether she overcomes her illness as you have asked or is bound for a heavenly destination, she is in good hands. Just believe that, and take comfort in knowing that His will be done."

"Deep down, I do believe in the righteousness of God's will," I said, "and I have an abiding faith. I simply need His comfort during this trying time. I also believe in miracles, and in the realization that many overcome fatal illnesses with His help … am I to believe in any less with regard to my Sara?"

With that said, he winked at me and said, "I probably shouldn't tell you this, but the fervent prayers from you and Linda have been heard and …" he glanced around as if he didn't want to be overheard "… I have it on good authority that good news awaits you later today."

And then John began fading from view. "Ooops, I guess someone up there heard what I said. I'll no doubt lose my head once again over that. Remember, you must always have faith! Believe!"

And with that he was gone. I moved closer to Sara's bed and took hold of her hand just as Linda walked in. "I think she's going to get better," I said. "I have this feeling that the worst of her illness is past and that she will be rejoining us soon."

Linda looked at me in awe, and said, "I sense the same thing. I just had the craziest dream. You were in it … and you were talking with one of the apostles … John the Baptist, I think … about Sara's recovery, and … why are you shaking your head? I'm not going crazy … it was just a dream!"

Sure enough, a few days later, Sara was home … running all around as if nothing had happened. I said a quick prayer thanking God for his mercy. "And," I said, "please forgive John for his little transgression. He meant well."

Slowly, our lives returned to normal, but with greater love for Sara than even I thought was possible. We were graced with two more children … another girl we named Carla and a boy we named Steve. My next encounter with a Spooky occurred when Carla was 4 years old.

Carla was a happy, exuberant little girl with pig-tails who desperately wanted to take piano lessons, and I

… wrestling with financial difficulties at the time … emphatically said "No". Well, Carla cried, her older sister called me a "bad daddy", Linda pleaded … but I was resolute. Seeing I was outnumbered, I quickly went out for a walk … thinking my absence would win the day.

I now realize that on this and other occasions where I held a minority opinion, absence only gives my worthy adversaries time to strategize on how 'daddy' could be 'manipulated' into changing his mind. Not a winning move on my part! But on this day, I needed time and a bit of fresh air to prepare for what I knew would be continued agitation.

I was so distracted by my thoughts on piano lessons that I didn't see the gentleman walking toward me, and only took notice when he stopped directly in my path. He was an older, slightly pudgy, man with a wild mop of greying hair. He wore a three button tweed coat with a puffy ascot and addressed me by name, which I thought was curious since I didn't recognize him. "Charles, you are most definitely wrong, and you need to arrange for piano lessons for Carla. A child's interest in music must be nurtured."

I glared at this stranger quizzically with resentment for his having butted into this decidedly personal matter. Angrily, I said. "Just who do you think you are to tell me how to rear my daughter. This is none of your affair!"

"My name is Ludwig," he said with a flair, "and

I know a thing or two about music. When I was Carla's age, I was already a prodigy on the keyboard … and I had a passion for the peace and satisfaction that music brought to my life. Carla could experience the same if given the chance, or she could lose forever the joy of music."

I stared at this odd looking gentleman, wondering why he looked familiar. Then it hit me. "Beethoven … Ludwig van Beethoven … that's who you remind me of."

"Well, I should remind you of him," he exclaimed. "That's exactly who I am. Virtuoso keyboardist extraordinaire … born in Bonn on March 16, 1770." He continued bragging about how influential he was to music, and ended up reminding me that he was "the greatest composer of all time."

We sat down together at a bus stop canopy. I realized by this time that this was a shadowy apparition from the past, just as Romeo and John the Baptist were several years earlier. But this was different. Not only was I seeing and talking with a spirit, but as we sat there, he began playing an imaginary keyboard and I could actually hear the music … the most beautiful and powerful Emperor Concerto.

As he played he looked over at me, and said, "Of all the music I wrote, this was my favorite. You know, it was first played in 1811 by Archduke Rudolf, my friend and patron in Vienna. I'll never forget that evening … even I sat mesmerized as he played, knowing this piece … my music … would be enjoyed long after my passing."

All of a sudden, he stopped playing and turned to face me … "The enjoyment of good music in children must not be discouraged. It offers a lifetime of tranquility and inner joy that sustains one through the most turbulent of times, and is a force for happiness in every aspect of one's life. Carla is asking … no, begging … you to give her the opportunity to enter the world of music that will become a solid foundation for her every future endeavor."

As I sat there contemplating what he had said, a bus rolled to a stop and several people got off. One older gentleman in a rather dated suit and tie came over and sat down beside us. "Hello, Ludwig. Is this the fellow who needs some help with his personal finances," he said pointing at me.

They obviously knew each other, and I seemed to be in the presence of another Spooky. Ludwig replied, "Yes. This is Charles and his little girl is asking for piano lessons and he can't seem to find the means to give her what she wants. You know me, Andrew, nothing is more important than music in one's life."

Andrew smiled knowingly at Ludwig and turned to me. He said, "Charles, I'm Andrew Mellon and I think we need to talk about the importance of budgeting, prioritizing and investing … the cornerstones of sound personal money management."

I thought to myself, "This is the man who created a vast business empire before entering politics as Secretary of the Treasury under Presidents Harding, Coolidge and Hoover. He presided over the boom years of the 1920s … and the Wall Street crash of 1929. Truly a legend in the world of high finance."

"I sense you know who I am," he said. "and I am aware of your struggles maintaining solvency for your family during these years of rapidly increasing demands and often insufficient growth of income. It's a balancing act … a common conundrum for young families."

He looked over at Ludwig, and said, "And you, Ludwig, need to have more compassion for our friend here. He has done well in providing for his family, and we should not be too critical." I nodded vigorously.

"But, Charles … don't lose sight of long term objectives when you prioritize your spending. There are some things that may seem unnecessary in the present that have great bearing on the future. Exposing your children to quality education and learning experiences are two of those. Ludwig is right in saying that Carla's interest in expanding her abilities in music should not be ignored."

I sat back and listened. It's not often you get free financial advice from a legend. Andrew continued, "Prioritizing in one's budget requires that you focus on what keeps your income rolling in, and budgeting involves covering essential living expenses, lifestyle expenses and future needs … living within your means while investing enough to meet your long-term goals. How you divvy up available revenue to meet those needs is the 'magic' you bring to your task."

As expected, he then noted the obvious … "Demands on your budget can be accommodated by either increasing income or reducing other expenditures."

Without hesitation, I responded, "I agree, but I seem to have reached a point where I've stretched the budget as far as possible. My prospect for increasing income is limited and expenses are very demanding."

"That's true," he responded, "but you can also look at alternative ways to obtain what you want. For instance, beginning piano lessons might be obtained from a neighbor or relative, or there may be options within the school system that could be explored.

"As an example, I knew a teller at one of my banks who desperately wanted to obtain tutoring for his child who wasn't doing well in school He didn't have the money needed, so he talked to a professor at the local college and offered to provide free bookkeeping services in his spare time if he would work with his child. Bartering enabled them both to get what they needed … problem solved."

As Andrew concluded his advice, I began to rethink

ways Clara might be accommodated. With that acknowledgement, Andrew began to fade from view. His last words were, "Don't forget, Charles, if something is important, there's always a way to find room in one's budget." Ludwig, looking on, winked and, with a twinkle in his eyes, also faded away.

Over the course of the last 13 years, I have had visits from several other Spooky's … and each time I benefited from our conversation. You might say that these spectral appearances have helped shape my life … and I'll be forever grateful for whatever in my psyche made me receptive to their apparition … be it the affliction of necromancy or that I'm a little bit crazy.

One of the more prominent Spooky's to come my way was Sam Walton … the visionary entrepreneur who founded WalMart … who chatted with me about his marketing philosophy on customer motivation.

And then there was Jim Thorpe … one of the most versatile American athletes in modern sports … a hero of mine who emphasized competition in all facets of life as the great motivator. And King Leonidas of Sparta … the leader of Greeks during the second Persian invasion as memorialized in the movie '300' … who strongly advocated to me the importance of physical training for mental acuity and tactical preparation for achieving one's objectives.

And I'll never forget having Mohammad Ali talking

with me about defensive patience as he demonstrated his 'rope-a-dope' strategy. Or the aroma of Winston Churchill's cigar as he talked about the power of oratory and its need for preparation. Or Clara Barton's smile as she quietly stressed the need for compassion for others and tender-loving-care for those in need. All of these Spooky's, as you can tell, made a lasting impression on me.

But the most impactful visit ... by far ... was my visit with Bob Hope. He appeared when I was unusually despondent ... trying to cope with the stress of an upcoming reassignment to WalMart International which would entail being on the road and away from home and family for much of the year.

As I was sitting on a park bench one afternoon ... feeling sorry for myself ... Mr. Hope approached me and said, "So, you'll be traveling? And just what are you moping about? I travel all the time, and I find it to be very rewarding."

*'I love flying. I've been to almost
as many places as my luggage'.*

That brought a smile to my lips. I immediately knew I was in the presence of a Spooky ... and said, "You're Bob Hope, aren't you?"

He looked at me in surprise, "You mean I have to confirm who I am?" He turned to show me his facial profile, "Doesn't this," he said, pointing to his silhouette, "convince you of who I am?

"And if that's not enough," he continued, "let me give you a few of my best one-liners.

On politics, *'No one party can fool all of the people all of the time; that's why we have two parties.'*

Or, *'I don't do a lot of political jokes. Too many are getting elected.'*

And, *'I don't know what people have against government, they haven't done anything.'*

My favorite: *'I always like to go to Washington, DC; it gives me a chance to visit my money.'*

Having died when I was 100 years old, you've got to be impressed with my sense of humor."

I relaxed a bit ... Bob Hope always made me laugh with his casual style and timely delivery, and being a Spooky didn't diminish his ability to entertain in a manner that didn't rely on racy language or divisional barbs.

"I also had a lot to say about aging," he continued:

'I can tell you how to stay young; hang around with older people.'

Or *'I'm so old, they've canceled my blood type.'*

Or *'I don't feel old. I don't feel anything till noon. That's when it's time for my nap.'*

And, *'You know when you're getting old; when the candles cost more than the cake.'*

"Ah, ha … I see a smile crossing your face," he noted. "I think you're learning something here. Humor is perhaps the most important trait in successful people … happy people. Look for the humor in everyday life and in the difficulties that pop up to ruin an otherwise good day. There's always something that will tickle your funny bone … in any situation.

"For instance, let's look at feminism,

'Where else but in America could the women's liberation movement take off their bras, then go on TV to complain about their lack of support?'

Or banking, *'A bank is a place that will lend you money if you can prove that you don't need it.'*

Or medicine, *'My next door neighbor just had a pacemaker installed. They're still working the bugs out, though. Every time he makes love, my garage door opens.'*

And golf, *'Golf is a game that needlessly prolongs the lives of some of our most useless citizens.'*

By this time, he had me laughing uproariously. My reassignment and traveling extensively looked less worrisome as I considered all the opportunities I'd have for taking my family … we could make this work for us, as a family.

Once again, Mr. Hope turned toward me and said, "Thanks for being a good audience. I hope you see how humor can help you make any situation better." With that, he did a little soft-shoe shuffle and faded away.

My memories of all the Spooky encounters I've had over the years have made a lasting impression, and I thank my lucky stars for each and every one. Those memories, you might say, have not only entertained me during difficult times, but they've taught me some valuable lessons on being who I am.

As Bob Hope would say,

"Thanks for the memory."

***

O is for

Odyssey

I'm not sure why I selected the word 'Odyssey' for this chapter in lieu of something like 'Overalls', 'Ovine', 'Oligarchy', or 'Onerous', but I did ... and I now find myself searching for a story line or two.

Perhaps I selected this word because we enjoyed many outings as a young family that might be considered family odysseys. I often hear our kids telling their kids about the weekends we spent driving several hours to take part in a volksmarch (a two hour, ten kilometer walk) in various locales and in often unfavorable weather. I'm not sure they really appreciated the long drives just to walk two hours for a collectible trinket. However, we all look back now on these forays as fond memories ... wondering what we're going to do with all those old medals and patches.

Or maybe because I really enjoyed reading Homer's Odyssey and it's tale of a warrior's 10 year travel home from the siege and conquest of Troy. His perilous journey and the various challenges he faced made reading the often stilted translation exciting to me in my younger years. The lure of ancient myths with their cast of overblown characters … the interaction with larger than life gods and demons … made the Odyssey hard to put down.

Or perhaps because I remember a vacation we took to Portland, Maine, when I was just a young lad, for some serious whale watching. We sailed into Casko Bay aboard the Odyssey, where the Captain guided us to see those magnificent mammals in their own environment. I still treasure the memories of frolicking whales, graceful harbor porpoises, high-flying seabirds, and a wide variety of other sea life we saw at play that day.

But for whatever reason, the word 'Odyssey' was selected for this chapter. As for story lines, I decided I'd focus on a present day 'warrior' … Al Delany … and his long trip home from Vietnam. His journey had eerie similarities to the saga of Odysseus … full of distractions and delays that made our hero's journey difficult. He, like Homer's hero, overcame all as a result of his abiding love of home and family.

Al's story is told below … both in prose and in verse … I couldn't make up my mind which to include, so you get them both. "So, Al … tell me about your Odyssey."

***

The Long Trip Home

My name is Al Delany. I have a tale to tell. It's about the challenges I faced returning home from Vietnam back in 1971. It was an odyssey. I had thought the travel home would be easy compared to the turmoils of serving a year in a war zone ... but it was not to be.

Like Odysseus who struggled finding his way back to Ithaca after a long war in Troy, I found my path home to be strewn with obstacles that made it a challenging trek. Not that I suffered the same calamities as he did, but I certainly didn't find the going easy. What drove me on during my odyssey was, like Odysseus, an abiding love of home and family.

I had a forewarning of sorts in my final days in Vietnam that my journey would not be easy. It happened on a clear evening as I walked from my living quarters to the mess hall for a late dinner. I passed by an old hag wearing a dark cloak sitting on a bench along the walkway seemingly deep in thought.

As I got closer, I noticed she was wearing a shiny amulet hanging on a gold chain around her neck. When I was within 3-4 feet of her bench, she suddenly jumped up and, staring directly at me, said, "Beware! The way is dark ... the road is bumpy ... the destination is fuzzy!"

At the time, I thought she had psychological problems caused by some kind of traumatic experience. But whatever, I didn't think much about it … perhaps I should have. As it turned out, my odyssey home was indeed dark, bumpy and occasionally directionless.

My year in Vietnam during the height of the war had many challenges. I was fortunate in having completed my tour with no lasting injuries or disorders … but that's a tale for another day. What made my time easier was that I was in Vietnam, not as a member of the military, but as a civilian supporting the military with the Army and Air Force Exchange System … AAFES … the BX/PX system.

My odyssey all started with a phone call from the Vietnam Regional Commander. "Son," Colonel Miller called everyone 'son', "It's time you got out of this god-forsaken country. I've just received orders for your reassignment to Fort Sam Houston in San Antonio, Texas.

"Get your things in order, pack your bags, and go to our logistics office at Tan Son Nhut airport at 0800 hours day after tomorrow … September 23rd. Sorry for the short notice, but I'd guess you don't mind the hurry-up. I'll send over your orders and all the authorizations you'll need."

I was able to complete my packing by the 23rd … a Herculean task considering the limited time I was given. You might say I needed no further

encouragement than ... "you're going home, son".
I only had two suitcases with personal things I
would be carrying with me ... and a briefcase with
papers and toiletries I would need in route. All other
belongings were packed and picked up for shipment
by cargo ship to San Antonio.

The Colonel's call couldn't have been more welcome.
I eagerly looked forward to rejoining my wife and
son, and arrived at the logistics office early. It was
then I encountered the first of the challenges I would
face on this odyssey. "Come on in, son," said the
elderly sergeant. This guy had obviously been with
Colonel Miller way too long.

He led me to a room with a table and two straight-
backed chairs ... and nothing else ... and motioned
me to sit. "You're Delany, right?" When I cautiously
nodded, he continued. "Well, I've got some bad
news ... and some worse news. But, on the plus side,
you're still going home.

"The bad news is your departure has been delayed
to the 28th. You'll have to twiddle your thumbs till
then. We've arranged for lodging at a nearby hotel,
but you're otherwise on your own." He grinned,
"As for the worse news, I'm afraid you're going to be
taking a boat to Hawaii and catching a plane from
there. We couldn't book you a seat on a contract air
carrier from here." I couldn't help but frown as I
shook his hand and walked out.

I lugged my carry-on luggage and hailed one of the

cabs roaming the airport. The driver helped stow my bags and I relaxed for what I thought would be a short ride to my hotel. An hour later, we stopped in front of what looked like a seedy apartment building … complete with a bright red, windowless door.

I got out of the cab, and while I was taking a more careful look at the 'hotel', the cab sped away with my two suitcases. I was left at the curb with only my briefcase. As I realized what was happening, I exclaimed, "To hell with it!" Frustrated, and in a sketchy part of Saigon, I simply waved 'goodbye' to my luggage and entered the 'hotel'.

I was sure that the taxi driver, who I had considered reputable, was by now haggling with a cohort about how much he might get for my belongings. To me, after a year in Vietnam, most of what was in my suitcases had long since outlived its value and was no great loss … but, the affront demanded I report the theft, knowing nothing would come of it … which I did … and nothing did.

The 'hotel' was indeed 'seedy', but it sufficed for the five days I was there while I collected what replacement items I needed for my trip home. My focus was on reuniting with Linda, my wife, and Danny, our son, and that made every stumbling block encountered seem easily surmountable. I'm sure those observing my smiling response to every difficulty wondered what I was on. If asked, I would have replied, "Love of family."

On the second evening at the hotel, I became somewhat restless and decided to venture out and get a drink. I found a nearby bar in what seemed to be a decent part of town after following several other Americans who looked like they knew where they were going. The bar was dimly lit and densely populated with various patrons enjoying an evening refreshment. As I settled in at the bar and took my first sip of a local beer, a big galoot ... tall and muscular for a Vietnamese ... approached me from behind, tapped me on my shoulder, and said in halting English, "You in my chair!"

Well, I motioned him to the empty stool to my right, and when he obviously thought the view from where I sat was more favorable, I moved to the empty chair myself. This fellow was big and menacing, and he obviously had a drink or two before I arrived. His pock marked face was accentuated with a black eye patch that covered his left eye, and the patch was adorned with the likeness of a skull, roughly drawn with bright red ink ... or was it blood?

"You making fun of Zhang?" he asked pointedly. I could immediately tell that Zhang was not one to be trifled with. I also decided he was Chinese, not Vietnamese. I refrained from asking if he liked chop suey, or some other conversation starter, and simply turned to talk with the young lady on the opposite side of where I now sat. She looked at the threatening character I was ignoring, said something undecipherable, and moved away. I think she was advising me that I might be in danger.

At that moment, I glanced over her shoulder and saw what I can only describe as a wizened old 'hag' wearing a dark floral cloak … she looked familiar … standing in the shadows by the door, grinning. A gem-encrusted amulet on a gold chain around her neck momentarily caught my eye just before my attention was once again … uncomfortably … drawn to my Chinese friend.

Zhang's hand grabbed my shoulder and spin me around. He moved close and stared ominously at me … the skull on his eye patch within inches of my face. He was obviously having difficulty seeing me with his one good eye. "Is there something I can do for you?" I asked cautiously, as I wondered how I might defuse the situation. "We seem to have gotten off on the wrong foot. If I have offended you in any way, I'm truly sorry."

With that said, Zhang made it evidently clear that he had to right a wrong … whatever that might be. He stood and I found myself, as I had many times during this grueling year, feeling I was in true danger. I slipped off my stool and ducked as his right fist sailed just short of my nose. It was then that one of the Americans I had followed into the bar approached and slung Zhang to the floor before he could wind up with another blow toward my as yet unbroken nose.

By this time, several other patrons came up and

stood with the American over this seemingly unpopular Chinaman. The bartender glared at the troublemaker on the ground with an M-16 resting easily within reach. Zhang had obviously not made many friends in this tavern and, realizing he was at a disadvantage, quickly rose and stumbled out of the bar.

"Hey, buddy," I said turning to my rescuer with great relief, "thanks for your help. I was pretty much expecting to become another notch in that guy's belt. By the way, my name's Al."

"No problem," the American said. He extended his hand in friendship. "My name's Rick. Us Americans need to look out for each other. I'm glad this situation was so easily resolved. I don't think he'll be any further trouble." I looked around to get a better look at the old woman who looked so familiar … but she was nowhere to be seen.

We strolled over to his table and he introduced me to his friends. "Al … this is Jerry and Dennis … we're just killing time waiting for our ship to sail. Heading home after a year with the 1st Infantry Division." We exchanged stories about our time in-country … their's being much more terrifying as they talked about chasing tunnel rats into their network of tunnels and facing the persistent firefights with the Viet Cong.

Dennis proudly lifted his pant leg to show me the scars he had from having stumbled onto hidden 'punji stakes' on one foray into the boonies. And Jerry … not wanting to be outdone … pulled open his shirt to show me the scar where a bullet had struck him in the left shoulder. "I didn't duck fast enough on this one."

My stories were tame in comparison, but just having been a part of the war effort and supporting America made us comrades. We continued rehashing memories and embellishing realities that were now a part of who we were.

As it turned out, the four of us were booked on the same ship to Hawaii, so we would continue our camaraderie on what would become a contentious trip subject to the whims of Mother Nature. You might say we established a bond, and that we looked forward to strengthening it in the days ahead.

When we parted late that evening and I walked back to my hotel, I felt a little better about the journey that lay ahead. It's always nice to share an experience with people you know … and like.

The next day, I awoke to a rapping on my door. I groggily made my way to the noise and was met by a Corporal in fatigues who said, "Al Delany? My name is Corporal Epstein. Colonel Miller has requested your presence, and I'm here to convey that request and drive you to his office." Well, at least he didn't call me 'son'!

After pulling on some clothes, Corporal Epstein

and I made the one hour trip back to the AAFES headquarters and I was immediately admitted to Colonel Miller's office. He reached over his desk to shake my hand in greeting and in his usual gruff voice said, "Good morning, son." I smiled and returned his greeting, forgoing the urge to call him 'dad'.

I sat in the chair facing his desk and he spoke at length about how I'd overcome tremendous obstacles in organizing the periodicals operation. Gone was talk about how happy I must be to leave this 'god-forsaken country' … he actually lowered his voice and soothingly talked in glowing terms about the benefits of being assigned to Vietnam and how it would advance my career in the years to come.

After laying it on a bit thick for the better part of 30 minutes, he finally came to what I assumed was the point of being called to his office. "Son, General Adams has called from Dallas" … he was the Commander of AAFES … "and he asked me to personally persuade you to stay on as the chief of our inventory management office. It'll mean a significant boost in your income, and a permanent promotion … but it'll also mean foregoing your trip home."

Well, this took me by surprise, and I was hesitant in answering. "Sir, this is something I need to think about … it impacts directly on my family and they need to be involved in my decision."

The allure of what he was suggesting was appealing,

and very seductive. But I also thought about how I yearned to rejoin Linda and Danny, and the joyful anticipation of being a family again that would be lost by accepting the tempting assignment. Income advantages, career opportunities, and job satisfaction … these were weighed against the risks of staying in Vietnam for another year, the loss of family time, and the negative impact of saying no to a personal request of the Commander of AAFES.

As I turned to leave, I hesitated and almost immediately turned back to face Colonel Miller. "I don't know why I'm delaying my response," I said. "I know right now my answer will be: NO! My time away from my family has been excruciating, and while I felt obligated to endure a year in Vietnam, I'm not interested in prolonging my time away from Linda and Danny. I must respectfully turn down your offer."

The Colonel looked pensive. "I understand your situation … and I've faced similar quandaries myself. But these are demanding times, and you're being asked to take on this assignment because you're the best person for the job. AAFES needs to take advantage of your experience and expertise right now … in this position. It would be a personal affront to turn your back on this opportunity. However, I've been authorized to sweeten the offer by making it a two-step promotion, with the corresponding increase in your salary, to make it more attractive to you."

"Colonel … it's not that the offer is unattractive … or that I don't recognize the advantages to my career and income that comes with it. I simply have other priorities … and returning to my family is foremost among those priorities. I sincerely appreciate the consideration given to me, but my answer is still: NO!"

Colonel Miller smiled, and said, "You know, son, between you and me you're making a wise decision. Don't tell anyone, but I'd probably do the same. I'll relay your preference in the best possible light, but don't be surprised if you continue to be enticed to accept this position as you get to Hawaii. They're going to continue with their sweet-talk and conniving ways to get you to accept, so be ready."

The following two days were fairly quiet while waiting for our departure. My three friends and I … the 'Four Horsemen' as we referred to ourselves … spent a lot of our downtime simply walking and talking … comparing histories. On the 28th, we boarded a swift boat at the Saigon port outside the small village of My Tho to begin our journey home. As we boarded, I thought I noticed down the pier a familiar figure … that old hag seen several times before … simply watching in the shadows as we pulled away from the dock.

This was my first experience on a swift boat, which were widely used to patrol coastal areas and interior waterways as a part of the 'brown-water navy'. It was an all-aluminum 50-foot long, shallow-draft vessel, and we zipped away from the dock and wound our way through the many moored boats in the harbor with surprising agility. As nimble as it was, however, I couldn't imagine it would be taking us all the way to Hawaii.

It wasn't long before I understood what was happening. We pulled along side what looked like a small aircraft carrier ... an LPH class ship equipped to carry helicopters: the USS Okinawa. We quickly scampered up the rope ladder deployed to bring us aboard and were greeted by Captain Bryson, the ship's commander. This would be our ride to Hawaii. We felt better being on a larger ship ... a decided advantage as we looked at the storm clouds gathering out at sea.

As we were escorted to our quarters, we learned the USS Okinawa had been built and commissioned in 1962 at the Philadelphia Naval Shipyard, and that it had since had a distinguished history of support in Korea and Vietnam. The seaman proudly noted that "a few months ago, we were awarded a citation by the President of the Philippines for the humanitarian assistance we provided to the people of Lagonoy Gulf who had been devastated by Typhoon Jean in October of last year."

Long after I arrived home, I learned that the USS Okinawa had gone on from dropping us off in Hawaii to be the recovery ship for the Apollo 15 space capsule and crew. I also heard that the ship had been decommissioned and unceremoniously sunk as a floating target in 2002 off the coast of Southern California. I hoisted a beer or two after learning the ship's fate and said a heartfelt goodbye to the USS Okinawa which had been my refuge on a harrowing trip home from Vietnam.

But, more about our trip, during which, like Odysseus, I fought my fear as Mother Nature focused her wrath on our path shortly after departing the protection of the harbor. The storm was furious and the winds howled. It was mid-day, but as dark as midnight, and the rain played its rat-a-tat-tat tune on the ships hull.

The waves slammed our transport and Captain Bryson's crew struggled to keep the ship facing into her fury. Was Mother Nature so insistent on preventing me from leaving Vietnam that she, like Poseidon, used her powers to thwart our passage? It sure seemed like it!

During the storm, we 'Four Horsemen' bravely huddled below deck in the safety of our quarters and talked incessantly just to calm our jittery nerves. Jerry stumbled several times to the latrine as his stomach made demands on his dignity and he up-chucked all that he had recently digested. Dennis for the most part lay quietly on his rocking bunk, trying to sleep through his fear that the ship was being threatened and we could do nothing about it … but pray for a quick end to its ravages.

Rick and I sat at a table and dealt numerous hands of poker with cards that seemed to take a life of their own as they flew from the table with each roll of the ship. We didn't pay any attention to the loss of cards … we didn't even know why we were playing … other than it was something to do while waiting for destiny to determine our fate.

During the height of the storm, a seaman, looking completely at ease as the ship lurched from one side to the other, stuck his head into our quarters … our refuge … as we sat there. "How goes it? The Captain said to let you know the worst of the storm has passed. We should see calmer sailing by morning." And he left snickering at our discomfort.

Well, the next few hours seemed just as turbulent as before our visitor had assured us the 'worst of the storm had passed'. We didn't sleep at all during the nightmarish tempest that raged all through the night. In fact, Rick and I followed Jerry to the latrine several times in the following hours … hoping that vomiting would calm our stomachs. Actually, we went not by choice … you might say we were compelled in response to the turbulent oceans. "OK, Mama Nature," I thought to myself. "You win! You're the boss out here!"

We did survive the night, but each of us swore that ocean sailings would never … ever … be a choice for us to get someplace. A vacation to Bali was definitely out!

When morning arrived, we had indeed outrun the worst of the storm. Three days later, we sailed into the Honolulu Harbor two days behind schedule as a result of our encounter with an angry Mother Nature. As we disembarked and walked down the dock into the customs area ... we gave thanks to be on solid ground once again.

Once inside, my friends were whisked away by their military handlers, and I was met by an AAFES representative who shepherded me through customs and into a waiting car.

After spending the afternoon at the AAFES Pacific headquarters being processed, I was ... as expected ... strongly encouraged to accept a continuation of my tour in Vietnam by the trio of executives with whom I met: the Director of Human Resources, the Manager of Inventory Management, and the Commander of AAFES Pacific. The enticements were clearly and forcefully laid out and I courteously and adamantly declined ... to all who would listen.

When the enticing allure of these modern day Sirens fell on deaf ears, I was quickly processed to continue my journey ... this time by plane to Everett, Washington ... en route to Texas. Upon arrival in Washington, I would rejoin Linda and Danny, who had been living there with Linda's parents.

Once again, however, fate intervened and the storm

which we had outran on the USS Okinawa, arrived with a pounding fury that shut down the Honolulu Airport for two days … my flight was cancelled. It seemed Mother Nature was not done with me yet. Subsequent bookings were quickly filled and I was not able to reschedule my journey till four days later.

So … another delay! What to do? I left the airport and decided to book lodging in the Ilikai Hotel which was an oceanfront high rise noted for appearing prominently in the opening credits of a favorite TV show … Hawaii Five-O. It was also located at the western end of Waikiki … a center for everything Hawaiian in Hawaii … and it was near Kuhio Avenue … best known for its restaurants, cafes, and night clubs. I should be able to find ways to occupy my time from there.

As I was checking in, I was pleasantly surprised to see my three buddies coming out of the elevator into the lobby … the Four Horsemen were together again. After exchanging greetings and getting caught up on our situations, they mentioned they were on their way to a luau. "You should come along," Rick said. "It'll be fun, and it'll help distract you from the delay in rejoining your family." How could I refuse. After all, we were the 'Four Horsemen'.

As we entered the Paradise Cove party site, we were each greeted in typical Hawaiian fashion … with a floral lei placed over our heads by a local beauty in a hand-painted sarong that easily accentuated her curvy body. The tropical Mai Tai we were handed and the traditional Hawaiian music that was ever present set the festive mood of the evening. The Four Horsemen were clearly in their element.

As we looked around at all the activities underway at the striking shoreline resort, we spotted a cabana along the path leading to the dining area. We were intrigued by a sign offering: 'Let Mordia tell your fortune for $10'. Well, being in transition to a new assignment, we all decided to see what the future had in store for us … our most recent past was not too memorable.

When my turn came around, I entered to see Mordia sitting at a round table with a glowing orb at its center. She was a mystical-looking older woman dressed in a white blouse with puffy sleeves wearing a dark floral cloak around her shoulders and having an intricate, gem-encrusted amulet dangling from a gold chain around her neck … she could very well have been a gypsy.

Mordia was just what I imagined a fortune teller would look like. At the same time, she looked very familiar. I was impressed and expected a convincing look into my future.

Mordia started by waving her hands over and around the globe, chanting something indecipherable. I grinned and successfully stifled a chuckle or two while thinking to myself, "This is the biggest waste of $10 I've ever laid out."

Finally, apparently speaking to hovering spirits, she
clearly said,

> "Oye … oye … I need your advice.
> Tell me what you see, and be precise.
> My friend is seeking a preview,
> Of his future endeavors to review.
> Give me a glimpse of what's in your sight,
> So his curiosity can be satisfied this night."

With that, she began mumbling again, and seemed
to be overcome by whatever she was experiencing.

After a few minutes of these gyrations, she was
abruptly flung back into her chair while letting out a
moan and gasping for air. Her eyes suddenly opened
wide and she stared at me with a troubled look. I
was seriously concerned for her well being and asked,
"Are you all right? What happened?"

Mordia slowly sat erect in her seat, regained her
composure and, still glaring in my direction, said in a
low, somber tone, "I see you have had a long journey
to these shores that seems to have been very difficult
… as if there were invisible forces plotting against
the completion of your travel." Hesitatingly, she
continued, "The spirits say that you will complete
your odyssey, but further travails will beset you."

She looked around and spoke of what the apparition
she alone had experienced told her. "This pause in
your journey will continue to pleasure you … for a
while. However, while you will be free from turmoil

on these isles, your three friends will vanish in a
mysterious manner. I see them ... then I don't ... I
see a shadowy presence of animals where once your
friends stood ... I sense their travels were preempted
in an unexpected manner."

At this point, she lapsed into quiet again, while she
seemingly listened to unheard voices ... then she
continued. "I also sense you have a sudden encounter
with ... I cannot tell what is met ... but I sense a loss
of control ... an upheaval ... and blood. You are not
alone, but your fate rests in your own hands. Take
care ... danger lies ahead!" Then Mordia slumped in
her chair and remained quiet for the remainder of
the session.

I exited Mordia's cabana and rejoined my waiting
companions. We walked on in silence toward our
table in the dining area. Once seated, we opened up
and jabbered uncontrollably about our experiences
with Mordia ... and the glimpses into our futures
that she foretold. Then, our attention turned
to the sights and aromas around us ... and her
prognostications seemed less important and were
soon forgotten.

We were regaled prior to the evening's entertainment
with an exceptional feast of delicacies. A Polynesian
buffet ... including pork cooked in the time-honored
Hawaiian manner: a kalua pig roasted in a traditional
rock-filled underground oven, unearthed in what
is known as an Imu ceremony. Once the pork was

brought out, a prayer to the ancient gods was offered and our feasting began.

"I may cancel my trip home," Rick said to me as he got up to refill his plate from the buffet table. "I'm sure my mom will understand. She may even want to join me in this Pacific paradise."

I smiled and quickly went with him to the buffet table. "Thanks for suggesting I join you … this is truly remarkable. That pork is the best I've ever eaten. What a contrast to our meals in Vietnam."

Just then, drums began a slow rhythmic beat and dancers appeared on the stage as ukuleles played a Polynesian melody. At one point in their performance, I was selected along with several other guests to learn the story-telling hula up on the stage … I was an embarrassing failure and I'm not sure what story my flailing arms and twisting body conveyed.

I awoke the next day dreamily reliving the previous evening in which we all enjoyed unbridled pleasures of our various senses. It was a beautiful morning as the sun was once again shining and soft breezes made strolling through Waikiki very pleasant. My thoughts again focused on Linda and Danny, and how I longed to be with them. "Two more days," I thought to myself, "and one relatively easy flight and I'll be home. I'm getting close!"

The four of us were to meet again in the Ilikai lobby

at 10:00. Rick had arranged with the USO for the four of us to tour some of the more rural areas around Honolulu. One of the sites visited on the bus tour was a working pineapple farm. Although not in season for harvesting, it was clear this crop was abundant as we drove through miles and miles of acreage with pineapple plants.

While there, we were given a history of how agriculture in Hawaii had changed from the old plantation days. It was interesting that this pineapple farm also had a pen of hogs that were raised to supply the Paradise Cove luau celebrations ... the famous pigs that were to be cooked in underground ovens.

I sort of stumbled on these pigs as I was looking for Rick and his friends. They had wandered off, and as I rounded a corner of the barn where one of the tour guides had said they had gone, I found pigs rummaging through their daily feeding. The guys were not there ... and I never saw them again. But off to my right, near the grove of trees in the distance, I noticed an older woman wearing a dark cloak ... what drew my attention was the glint of a gem-encrusted amulet dangling from a gold chain around her neck.

"All right," I said to myself, "I know you're thinking that in the Greek version of the Odyssey, the witch-goddess Circe had turned Odysseus' crew into swine. Could this woman in the distance be Mordia ... my

equivalent of Circe? Could my friends have been
…..?"

As exciting as that might have been, Rick, Jerry and
Dennis had not been magically turned into pigs.
I found out later that a military adjutant from the
local logistic office had found them and taken them
back to the hotel to pack. They had been rescheduled
onto a flight that was leaving that afternoon.
Time was lacking for them to alert me to the
change in their plans. But I will never look at pigs
again without thinking of my friends … the Four
Horsemen … who were hence no more.

Early the next morning, I gathered my belongings
and took a taxi to the airport for the continuation
of my journey home. I smiled a lot that morning in
anticipation of soon being reunited with Linda and
Danny. My Continental Airline flight would take
approximately 7 hours and I anticipated arriving
shortly before 4:00 that afternoon. It looked like my
grueling odyssey was nearing its conclusion.

The Honolulu International Airport was busy, but I
… surprisingly … encountered no further delays. We
departed on time, and landed at the Seattle-Tacoma
International Airport in a heavy storm of rain and
sleet. It seems that Mother Nature's storm that we
battled several days earlier on the USS Okinawa, had
made it to the west coast before I did. Once I cleared
customs and security, I made my way to the baggage
claim area, and was met there by Linda's dad, Jeff.

"How're ya doing, son," he exclaimed with a big smile. It seems I have this affect on people ... I'm everyone's 'son'. At least I really was Jeff's son (in-law) and I couldn't blame Colonel Miller. We exchanged greetings and withstood the crush of travelers making their way to the baggage claim area. "Let's get your luggage and get on home, before it gets any colder out there."

As was fitting for this difficult journey, it did not surprise me when my luggage failed to appear and we had to leave with assurances from the airline representative, "Don't worry. We'll find your bags and deliver them to your home. Nothing gets truly lost in this day and age."

I wasn't so sure, but we departed and made it to Jeff's car without further ado. "How'd you like to drive? You haven't forgotten how, have you?" It seemed he knew full well that I always preferred to drive, so I agreed and got behind the steering wheel.

The roads had been pretty well cleared of snow and they had been liberally treated with a salt solution, but I cautiously made my way out of the airport and onto the streets heading to my reunion with Linda and Danny. Driving was not a problem ... that is until I arrived at a bridge crossing an inlet of Puget Sound. Mother Nature had one last shot at this wearisome traveller.

I cautiously approached the bridge knowing intellectually that ice tends to form earlier and last longer on overpasses. Being a southern boy, however, I was, perhaps, over confident since my driving experience had been predominantly on ice-free surfaces … I was more accustomed to hurricanes, tornados, and flash floods. Jeff was looking apprehensively at the bridge ahead and was beginning to warn me of the icy conditions when off to my right I spied a familiar sight.

"Do you see her?" I shouted. "There … on the shoulder?" In the split second I was distracted by what I thought I saw before my gaze returned to the road ahead, the car was on the bridge … hit an icy patch … and began skidding toward the bridge railing. The impact was sudden, and the car spun around three or four times before coming to a stop in the middle of the road. Fortunately, I was driving slowly and there was no other traffic, so the damage was limited to what had been inflicted by the bridge encounter … seemingly rather minor … but my pride was seriously eroded.

As Jeff and I opened our eyes and surveyed the situation, we reassured each other that we had survived. The car had sustained a badly dented front fender, but all else seemed to be OK. Jeff seemed to be OK, but my lip had made contact with the steering wheel and had begun bleeding. I dabbed at my lip to staunch the flow of blood and slowly restarted the car. With my bleeding lip under control, I cautiously drove off the bridge to the side of the road where we could take a closer look at the drivability of the car.

"What did you see, back there?" Jeff asked. "You were yelling something about someone standing on the roadway."

Recalling those seconds before the spin, I looked back to where I had been distracted. Seeing nothing, I said, "I'm not sure what I saw. I thought there was an old woman on the road wearing a dark cloak ... she looked familiar in the fading evening light."

I recounted my visit with Mordia in Honolulu and her previous sightings. "And like those other appearances, she just disappeared tonight as quickly as she had appeared. What had drawn my attention this time was the glint of that same gem-encrusted amulet I had seen before." In the meanwhile, I was thinking, "Boy, that's the way to really impress your father-in-law!"

Jeff shook his head in wonder, and immediately changed the subject. "Well, let's get this car moving. We have loved one's waiting for us."

In spite of the mishap and resulting blemish on my bragging rights as a skilled driver, Jeff didn't hesitate on having me drive the rest of the way. I'll forever be grateful for his confidence ... however, the car exhibited the true story.

Linda and Danny were standing in the doorway as we drove up, and they both ran toward the car as I rolled to a stop. Grinning from ear-to-ear, I jumped out and embraced them in the biggest family bear hug ever, and thought to myself, "I'm finally where I'm supposed to be."

As the welcoming greetings came to an end, and we all moved into the house, I gave a quick "Thank you" to my guardian angels for getting me this far. Then, Linda lovingly took a Kleenex and dabbed at the trickle of blood oozing from my split lip.

She gave me a sidelong glance as she said, "Hmmm. A dented car … a bloody lip … a very generous hug. I can hardly wait to hear about the adventures you had on your odyssey home!" When we were comfortably seated, I turned to them all and began my tale of the obstacles I had to avoid on my way home.

"You won't believe all I've had to endure. This has been a journey I thought would never end. It all began just after learning I would be transferred to Texas when I was walking to the officer's mess one evening and an old crone sitting on a bench jumped up and startled me. She stared in my direction, pointed directly at me with her gnarled finger, and said, 'Beware! The way is dark … the road is bumpy … the destination is fuzzy!' It couldn't have been more prophetic!

"So, sit back and let me spin my tale … I call it: 'A Modern Day Odyssey'."

***

A Modern Day Odyssey

Herein is my recounting of days gone by
When I journeyed from conflict and death
A convoluted route to my family faraway.

My field of conflict was battle-torn Nam
A year supporting our troops at war…
Logistical and security challenges in play.

Like Odysseus, my trek home encountered
A host of dangers, distractions and delays…
All manner of obstacles to hinder each day.

> *Odysseus, like me, was compelled by*
> *His abiding love of home and family!*

The difficulties to be encountered
Should not have been a surprise…
A hag's warning cast the future as dark gray

She jumped up along my path and
Pointed directly at me, saying: "beware"…
"A dark and bumpy road will hinder your way."

I learned her name was Mordia, and
A shiny amulet hung around her neck…
She oft was there when times were in disarray.

> *Mordia's foreboding was countered by*
> *My abiding love of home and family.*

My orders for leaving the strife behind
Were delayed … and delayed again…
Repeated challenges held me at bay.

Finally, after rescheduling found a way,
My journey began and optimism reigned...
But a promising start was soon to go astray.

A dark and bumpy journey followed
With my resolve too often at risk...
A comparison to the Odyssey on full display.

> *Patience was needed, but I relied on*
> *My abiding love of home and family!*

Ere my departure, a one eyed Chinaman,
Akin to the Cyclops faced by Odysseus ...
Threatened danger to my life in every way.

A flying fist painfully struck my waiting cheek,
Sending me sprawling, my eyes blurring...
Friends rallied to defend and saved the day.

Obviously not in control, outnumbered,
His one eye darted to find an out...
My nemesis departed, a coward running away.

> *One less danger to hamper*
> *My abiding love of home and family.*

Attractive enticements to remain were offered...
The 'Sirens' call to thwart my homeward travel...
But a more rewarding destiny was underway.

Wealth and position were put before me
But they were no reason for me to delay...
My response was a resounding: 'no way'!

Temptations earnestly offered failed,
I was resolved to abandon this land of strife...
Offerings ended being no temptation that day.

> *Nothing could prevail over*
> *My abiding love of home and family!*

Seats on air transport were not to be had,
Thus travel part way by ship was endured...
A slower solution, but I was on my way.

However, Mother Nature had other plans and,
Like Poseidon, she furiously imposed her will...
Storms rocked our journey and sent us astray.

But the captain held firm and steadfastly
Guided us through the storm's worst...
Fear of death passed with the light of a new day.

> *Even Mother Nature could not overcome*
> *My abiding love of home and family.*

Arriving in the land of luau's and lei's
My journey continued to be plagued...
But again and again, my will held sway.

The siren's call of wealth and promotion
Were intensified by command to no avail...
My image of wife and child a mainstay.

Even threats of a less favorable future
Only made other options more tempting...
My mind was focused on a homeward way.

> *Career was no longer a factor... only*
> *My abiding love of home and family.*

Three friends and I explored the island
And found sights and a luau enticing…
Grass skirts swung freely as faded the day.

My attempts to master the hula failed
And I blushed as the audience laughed…
All soon forgotten when dining was underway.

A Polynesian buffet was served with
A Kalua pig unearthed … a feast for sure…
A most memorable way to conclude our stay.

> *But, delicacies aplenty did not deter*
> *My abiding love of home and family.*

While there, I was drawn to a cabana,
By a sign reading: 'Mordia Sees Your Future'…
I entered to have my future surveyed.

Inside, Mordia hovered over a glowing globe
Dressed as I imagined a fortune teller would…
She appeared and let spirits have their say.

She spoke of my perilous journey, and
Of friends vanishing and a bloody encounter…
However, forecasts of gloom turned out okay.

> *It only confirmed nothing is more real than*
> *An abiding love of home and family.*

Fear arose when my friends vanished
And three pigs appeared where they had been…
Akin to Circe's 'crew-turned-to-swine' cliche.

Could it be that classical myths were real
And Circe's curse befell my three friends…
Did Mordia's vision come into play?

No … they simply gained an early flight
And were whisked away to their plane…
Their homeward trek was underway.

> *My friends leaving only showed*
> *Their abiding love of home and family.*

Finally, my flight was wings-up with
A stateside landing soon upon me…
My father-in-law welcomed me to the USA.

The weather was cold and sleeting,
Thus delaying a reunion with wife and son…
They remained home out of harms way.

It was 35 miles to the long awaited reunion,
And enjoying the chance, I chose to drive…
But fate once again blocked our way.

> *I marveled anew at the value of*
> *My abiding love of home and family.*

An icy patch on a bridge-crossing
Caused the car to skid and spin…
Into the bridge rail our car did stray.

Though the car was thusly redecorated
With dents, scrapes and a front defaced…
It survived to carry us the remaining way

My wife and son rushed to greet us,
As we drove up and parked at her door…
Happiness was once again a mainstay.

Holding each other, I celebrated
My abiding love of home and family.

Though Mordia envisioned dire events,
And seemed to appear ominously en route…
My imagination was clearly in play.

Friends were not turned into pigs,
And my bloody lip was hardly dire…
Mordia's warnings clearly went astray.

Was it simply my anxiety to get home,
Or a dread of the challenging trek?
Whatever … it was all worth it this day!

I believe true happiness ever relies on
An abiding love of home and family!

So my odyssey from the perils abroad
Was often challenging … but for naught…
Our family reunion made me yell: 'HOORAY'!

The moral of this tale is simply this:
'Nothing can be daunting when you have
An abiding love of home and family!'

***

P is for
Paladin

After considering other options, I settled on using the word 'Paladin' when I got to the 'P' chapter. It's a good word, used sparingly today, but full of story telling possibilities.

The word Paladin is usually defined as 'a champion of a cause'. Because of its French roots, however, Paladin is often interpreted to be a warrior. As an example, the 12 knights in attendance to Charlemagne were called Paladins.

As time went on, its meaning grew to include any chivalrous or heroic person.

The idea of there being a force for good… available to right wrongs … has always appealed to me. As a result, the old TV show 'Have Gun, Will Travel', and its hero, Paladin, became a favorite during my early years.

Even though Paladin seemed to be a run-of-the-mill mercenary … offering his chivalrous services for a $1,000 fee … he quite often came to the aid of desperate folks without compensation. The word also has other usages, and is, therefore, chosen as an interesting word to explore in this chapter.

———————-

While considering what I should write for this chapter, a good friend introduced me to the challenge of writing stories within a 101 word limit. Although I am clearly a novice in that writing style, I thought it would be interesting to write tales in that manner for this chapter.

So, here are my tales spun around he word 'Paladin' … written within a 101 word constraint. And … as a bonus … a more lengthy tale about the Paladin of TV fame that you may not have heard before … it closes out this chapter.

***

My Hero

I walked into the tavern I last visited with Grandpa Scott when I was five. He would set me atop the well-worn bar as he chatted with his buddies.

There ... sitting quietly ... I wondered if this was how it was in the days of 'Have Gun, Will Travel' ... my favorite TV show. They chatted about this and that ... emphasizing the humor in everyday situations.

I now sat quietly on a stool near the spot I had earlier perched, remembering how much I revered Grandpa ... my hero ... the Paladin of my world.

His had been a sorrowful funeral!

***

The Chessman

The stranger, talking seriously with my dad, displayed a card saying simply, "Have Gun, Will Travel". The image on the card … a chess knight … matched the silver emblem on the holster hanging at his hip.

"Mr. Paladin, will you help my dad," I asked with all the brashness of my 6 years?

He replied, "Yes."

"Do you use silver bullets?"

"No."

"Have a talented horse like Trigger?"

"No."

"Can you sing a ballad?"

"No."

"Do you have a marshal's badge?"

"No."

"Do you……."

"Hold on there, son. I'm only here for a game of chess with your dad."

***

The Emissary

The Paladin arrived during the harvest of 802. As the emissary of Charlemagne, his word was law and we greeted him with due reverence.

"Why are you here," asked the village elder.

He replied, "To make your village great again!"

"But we have always been a poor agrarian community ... never great."

"Ah, that is about to change," he responded.

Looking suspiciously at the Paladin, he said, "Will we like the change?"

"Do you like prosperity?"

"Yes!"

"Then welcome to the world of Charlemagne ... all is possible."

Four years later, during a meager harvest, a new Paladin arrived ... promising greatness.

***

The Question

In my history class, we're studying Charlemagne. I marveled at the way he united Western Europe ... his Paladins were chivalrous agents spreading the Holy Roman Empire's doctrine.

Leaving class one day, I heard a question from behind ... "Are you a Paladin?"

Turning, I met the gaze of an attractive coed I had admired in class ... her beautiful green eyes twinkling. "Well, are you a Paladin?"

"I feel I am now," I replied, as my chest swelled and past hesitations to approach her were forgotten. "I am definitely ready for a little unity. How about a soda?"

***

Satisfaction

In the background, was a familiar refrain …

> ♪ *Paladin, Paladin, where do you roam?*

… and our favorite TV show captivated all.

> ♪ *Paladin, Paladin, far, far from home.*

I quietly moved through the house …

> ♪ *He travels on to wherever he must;*

… and my destination loomed …

> ♪ *A chess knight of silver his badge of trust.*

… with no naysayers in sight.

> ♪ *There are campfire legends the plainsmen spin*

Dieting would soon be forgotten …

> ♪ *Of the man with the gun,*

… and a big slice of chocolate cake …

> ♪ *of the man called Paladin.*

… would be mine!

***

The Cure

The Coronavirus swept across our town like a wildfire. Half the population tested positive and deaths were rising. Drastic action was called for, and I was ready.

I poured half a glass of Bombay Sapphire, adding ice and tonic, and took my first sip. This was my way of fighting this pandemic … my bulwark … better than a troop of warriors. I call this my Paladin.

If only my neighbors had enlisted my Paladins. The pandemic scare would become less important. Tranquility would return to our town.

But then, who needs a pandemic to enjoy a Bombay and tonic.

***

Enough of the short stuff. Here's an extended tale about Joey Starrett, the boy from 'Shane', and his evolution to becoming Paladin, the man from 'Have Gun, Will Travel' fame ... the early years that helped shape his legend.

This is a 'what might have been' tale that brings forward many of the heroes of my youth. Wouldn't it have been interesting if these bigger than life characters were real and the adventures portrayed were as exciting as I envisioned them to be?

***

The Man in Black

Joey ran across the field after the man riding off toward hills in the distance, yelling "Shane, come back! Shane ... Shane!" But this man, who had heroically stood tall against the intimidation of the local cattle baron and his ruffians, rode off without acknowledging Joey's pleas.

Now you may be familiar with the story of young Joey's attachment to a man named Shane, but have you ever wondered what became of Joey? Well, that's the gist of this tale. How does this relate to 'Paladin'? Read on ... all will be explained.

First off, you need to know that Joey's family, the Starrett's, didn't stay in Wyoming ... they moved to San Francisco after deciding that scratching a living

out of their unforgiving homestead was a lost cause.
Joey's father became a merchant and they lived a
good life in the bay area.

When we pick up on Joey's story, 12 years have
passed and he is no longer the boy who chased after
Shane. He had become a young man of wealth
and stature as an outgrowth of their move to San
Francisco and to his penchant for the finer things
available in the big city … and, not unrelated, to a
successful series of high stakes poker games.

His residence was now the Hotel Carlton and
he was frequently seen around town dressed in a
'gentleman's' attire, and he commanded the respect
of both friends and strangers. He was at ease with his
life, but he never forgot the man who had made such
an impression in his youth.

Shane was a role model, and Joey had decided to
use his new-found wealth and stature to aid the
less fortunate whenever possible, just as Shane had
done for his parents. To that end, he developed an
alternate persona when he was called upon to right
wrongs that beset people in trouble.

Joey trained himself in preparation for situations
he might encounter pursuing this endeavor. He
strengthened his body and practiced the physical arts
… he became a master of firearms, both pistols and
long guns, and skilled in the fast draw … he adopted

a calm demeanor that allowed him to quickly evaluate dangerous situations ... and he became adept at reasoning with people. All in all, he became a force to be reckoned with.

He also changed his appearance in these instances to be more reflective of his role as an enforcer for the troubled ... most noticeable were his black Stetson with a silver band around the crown, and a six-shooter hanging at his waist with a silver knight chess piece on its holster.

He introduced himself as Paladin and he was quite impressive in his jet black getup ... some may even say he looked fearsome. He was often referred to as the 'man in black'.

He even created calling cards with the insignia he adopted (a silver knight chess piece) promoting his services. They included the phrase 'Have Gun, Will Travel', along with his telegraph address.

He passed these out liberally thinking that once people knew he was available to assist with their problems, they would turn to him when troubles descended. He would thus be able to provide the help reflective of the aid Shane gave his family.

Initially, he found very few causes in his home town that required his help. That surprised him ... San Francisco during his time was not exactly known for being a bastion of respectability.

Perhaps the dark image he created caused potential

clients to be as fearful of him as they were of their own demons, but local opportunities to showcase his services were not forthcoming. Or maybe it was that he asked for a $1,000 gratuity for his services.

In any case, the man in black eventually decided to respond to several requests for help he received from people further away. Those causes were more often a matter of life and death, and their need was such that all hesitations to 'hiring' Paladin faded.

He gathered himself up, becoming the man of distinguished courage and ability, who would be admired for his brave deeds and noble qualities … or so he hoped. He became Paladin.

Exhibiting exceptional seriousness, he mounted his horse, a jet black stallion named Rafter, and set off on his quest to help those in need.

His initial destination was Tombstone, Arizona. It seemed that a gang of outlaws calling themselves the 'Cowboys', led by the Clanton brothers, were menacing local ranchers in the area. They rustled cattle and were causing general mayhem when they came into town. It had turned serious when ranch hands were being killed. Several local residents had written and seemed desperate to have Paladin's help.

"Well, Rafter, it looks like we have ourselves a mission," Paladin said reflectively as they headed out of the city. "Tombstone awaits!"

Stopping for the night along a stream in southern California, he had a bite to eat and was relaxing by the fire when a traveller heading north approached. "Howdy," the stranger said. "Just passing through … any troubles along the road ahead?"

"None that I encountered," Paladin replied.

As the visitor looked quizzically at Paladin, he asked, "Are you that fella they call Zorro. I hear he wears a black outfit like you and is known to frequent these parts."

Paladin grinned, and responded, "Nope. But I hear he's a force for good for people hereabouts. Sort of a Robin Hood … you know, helping those who are ill equipped to help themselves. Won't you join me by the fire?"

"No, thanks … I need to be on my way. They say Zorro wears a mask, so I should have known you weren't him." The stranger then turned to leave.

"I may not be Zorro," Paladin said to his departing visitor. "But I do hope to be of help to others along my road ahead." He reached out and gave him his calling card. "Travel safely."

The next morning, he and Rafter continued their journey. It took Paladin another two days to reach Tombstone, and when he rode in, everything was quiet. He headed for the livery stable and told the keeper to feed and water Rafter "with the best you got."

They chatted for a while, and Paladin asked, "It seems awfully quiet here. I heard that the Clanton brothers were causing a lot of havoc in the area. I was a little worried I might encounter some troubles when I rode in, but there's no sign of anything amiss."

"Well, mister," the liveryman replied. "You just missed all the excitement. There was a big showdown just two days ago … right outside in the corral … when the marshal and his brothers outgunned the Clanton gang.

"Yep. Wyatt, Virgil and Morgan Earp, together with Doc Holliday … they had enough of the feuding with those rascals and finally called them out. They met here at the OK Corral and after all the gun fire ended, Billy Clanton and both Tom and Frank McLaury were dead."

He went on to tell Paladin that Virgil, Morgan and Doc Holliday were wounded, but not seriously, "so, I guess you could say the Cowboys lost the battle of the Gunfight at the OK Corral.

"However, I expect Ike Clanton, Billy Claiborne and Wes Fuller ran off just so they could fight another day. It's said that Ike hobbled down the road like a six year-old playing hopscotch and Billy and Wes were screaming like banshees as they raced away, bobbing and weaving. However, they ain't ones to forgive and forget, and the Earps haven't seen the last of them. But for now, all is quiet."

As Paladin thought of how this development affected his mission, he walked down the road to the doctor's office. Doctor Martin had been one of the townsmen who had written, pleading for Paladin to come to their aid. He insisted that Tombstone was rapidly growing, and that the arrival of womenfolk and churches would only continue if peace and stability prevailed.

When he entered, Doc Martin was in the outer room talking with a patient who was just leaving. Paladin introduced himself, and said, "I understand that the situation you were concerned about may have been resolved. With three of the outlaw band dead and the others scattered, you may no longer be fearful of their shenanigans."

Doc Martin nodded, as Paladin continued. "It seems that my services are no longer needed. I just stopped by to let you know that I arrived and that I'm going to keep riding. I've got a situation over in the New Mexico territory that needs my attention."

Paladin turned to leave, but as an afterthought, he reached out and gave Doctor Martin one of his calling cards. "Just in case those boys start acting up again, let me know and I'll return," he said, closing the door behind him.

Once again, Paladin mounted Rafter and they moseyed out of town. "Well, Rafter, I'm glad to see there's a number of gallant men around who will take charge of bad situations, but it sure lessens the need for my services."

Looking ahead, Paladin thought of the letter he had received from Amy, the new wife of Will Kane, a man of principal Joey had met while still in the Wyoming territory before his family moved to San Francisco.

According to her letter, Will was currently the sheriff in Hadleyville in the New Mexico territory. She was anticipating his retirement from sheriffing and their looking ahead to a new life as a store owner in another town, but the tone of the letter was fearful.

He recollected the words she wrote: "An outlaw Will captured years ago, Frank Miller, is being released from prison and has said he would be heading our direction. Apparently he blames Will for his incarceration and he's revenge driven."

Without directly asking, Paladin understood that she was afraid Will would delay their departure out of a sense of duty to face Miller … and that she would appreciate his help. "We'd better get a moving, Rafter. We need to get to Hadleyville before Miller's arrival if we're going to be of any help."

Two days later, they arrived at their destination.

Everything seemed calm as he rode toward the little house on the edge of town that Amy Kane had said was their home. When no one answered his knock, he turned to leave and a neighbor came out to ask, "Anything I can do for you, stranger?"

"Just looking for Amy or Will Kane," he said looking intently at this older, wizened man. "Know where I might find them?"

The neighbor looked at the man in black suspiciously, and said, "You just missed them. Will's retired and they left on the morning train for a new life in Edgerton. They'll open a store there."

Paladin smiled, "Well, I'm happy their new life together is getting off to a good start. But I heard that a no-good named Frank Miller was coming to seek payback for prison time he served. Did he ever show up?"

"You bet he did, and he brought three rogues with him. They had a face-off yesterday just down Main Street. Will stood tall and took them all on. To our shame, no one came out to help him … by golly, he faced them alone and protected our town … only Amy gave a damn. The town's a bunch of cowards who let Will and Amy fend for themselves.

"When the shooting was done, and Miller and his gang were laying dead in the dirt, the townsfolk all came out to pat him on the back, telling him how proud they were of him. But Will just looked around at them, dropped his badge on the ground and walked away with his arm around Amy ... they were all hypocrites ... not a proud day for Hadleyville!"

Paladin stood quietly thinking of his friend Will, and then said to the neighbor, "I'm sorry I arrived too late to offer my help. Will's a good man who would never back down from protecting his town ... and he should never have had to meet this challenge alone. It's good that he and Amy are out of here."

The neighbor nodded, thinking to himself, "This stranger is rightly criticising the town ... and me, as well." He looked away and shuffled in the dirt ... his embarrassment very evident.

The man in black pulled a calling card from his pocket and handed it to the man looking anywhere but at him. Paladin was sorely tempted to tear it in half and throw it on the ground. "I usually give out my card to folks in case I might be able to help in some way. But I'm not so sure this town is ready to be helped. So, don't call me unless the town has shown they're willing to help themselves.

He turned, got back on Rafter and slowly rode out of town. "Come on, boy. We've been in Hadleyville too long."

His next destination was Dodge City, Kansas. He had received word that it had become a boomtown as a result of its becoming the destination for Texas cattle drives coming north along the Great Western Cattle Trail. It was known as the 'queen of the cow towns'.

The growth of the town brought a degree of civilization to the Kansas plains, but the conglomeration of people with newly acquired wealth also attracted those wanting to make an easy buck in less legitimate ways.

In Paladin's mind, this meant there would be more than a few who could use his help. So, he and Rafter headed for Dodge City.

As he was riding through Texas, he made a stop in Abilene prior to getting on the cattle trail north. The few scattered buildings there were not impressive and Paladin thought to himself, "Well, Rafter, let's just get a few supplies and keep moving north. Nothing much of interest here."

He stopped at the local general store and dismounted at the rail out front where two other horses were tied. Both of these horses were of superior stock ... one a golden palomino with a long white mane and the other a snow white stallion with a fancy saddle trimmed with silver elements. Paladin smiled as he stroked first one and then the other.

As he moved to enter the store, the merchant came out talking with a stranger wearing a mask. As they ended their conversation, the merchant waved and the masked man mounted the white stallion and

rode off in a cloud of dust and thundering hoofbeats.
It seemed Paladin could hear the man yell as he rode
off, "Come on, Silver! Let's go, big fellow! Hi-yo
Silver! Away!"

Paladin turned to the merchant and asked, "Who
was that masked man?"

In response, the merchant said, "That was an old
friend I only know as the Lone Ranger. He just
turned a trio of bad fellas in to the sheriff and
stopped by to say hello. By the way, my name's
Murphy."

As he stood there watching the Lone Ranger ride off,
he heard the picking of a guitar from the inside the
saloon next door to the general store. Then a voice
began singing:

> *"Oh, give me land, lots of land under starry skies above*
> *Don't fence me in.*
> *Let me ride through the wild open country that I love*
> *Don't fence me in!*

> *Let me be by myself in the evening breeze,*
> *Listen to the murmur of the cottonwood trees,*
> *Send me off forever, but I ask you please*
> *Don't fence me in!*

> *Just turn me loose, let me straddle my old saddle*
> *Underneath the western skies*
> *On my cayuse, let me wander over yonder*
> *Till I see the mountains rise"*

After listening for a while, Paladin gave the store keeper a surprised look. "That cowboy's got a pretty good voice."

"Yep," Murphy responded, "and he can yodel, too. He's the owner of that palomino there … name of Roy Rogers … and the horse is Trigger … the smartest horse I've ever seen. He's passing through on the way to his ranch down near Fort Worth.

"Apparently," Murphy continued, "he's been helping the territorial marshal round up a bunch of rustlers who have been plaguing ranches around here. Got em, too!"

"Hmmm," the man in black thought to himself. "Two more men of courage out to rid the area of those intent on taking advantage of others. Shane's not the only good samaritan out here "

Paladin walked into the store with Murphy and gathered up what he needed. On his way out, he turned and shook the merchants hand. "Murphy … here's my card. I like to be of help to people in difficult situations. It looks like you've got everything under control here, but send for me if my services are ever needed."

With that, he stowed the supplies just purchased, mounted Rafter, and rode out of Abilene.

Passing through the Oklahoma territory on his

way to Dodge City he made a stop in the town of McLintock. This town was well known to cattlemen … it was named after George Washington McLintock, or GW to his friends, a larger than life rancher who had over the years tamed this territory with a firm hand and fair justice for all … including local Indian tribes.

McLintock's ranch included acreage that stretched for miles in the southern Oklahoma territory, and his herds of cattle were a major source of beef for people in all directions. He had earned a well deserved reputation for being a benevolent force in the 'wild west'.

The morning train was just pulling in, and Paladin stopped at the station and joined the large crowd that had gathered. It turned out that Chief Puma of the Comanche tribe was arriving after having been released from prison. He and McLintock had engaged in many struggles over the years, but now shared a mutual respect and friendship.

Puma was here to represent the Comanche who were facing the eviction from their tribal lands, which were desired by the territorial governor, to be herded onto a reservation near Fort Sill. Puma asked that McLintock be their spokesman at the hearings later that day.

Paladin saw that McLintock greeted Puma warmly and said, "I'd be honored to speak for the Comanche. Just give me the words and I'll translate your views so that all understand your side in this struggle."

It was said that McLintock didn't care much for the territorial governor, Cuthbert H. Humphrey, and minced no words in his interactions with him. At one point, when someone had called the governor a gentleman, GW blurted out, "He'd have to be a man first before he's a gentleman, and he misses on both counts."

Paladin was impressed that two long time enemies had overcome their bitterness and forged a bond that transcended their differences.

The man in black approached GW before the hearing and said, "My name's Paladin, and I just wanted to shake your hand. You're one of quite a few men I've met wandering the frontier who are helping to bring civilization to this land."

Before departing, Paladin stopped at the local sheriff's office and dropped off one of his calling cards. "Just in case you need help at some point down the line," he said to the deputy sitting at a desk, "this is how you can reach me. However, with GW around, I seriously doubt my help will be needed."

That having been completed, he once again mounted Rafter and headed north to Dodge City.

He arrived at his destination the next day, and

decided he'd stop in at the Long Branch Saloon, a well attended drinking establishment near the center of town. For all its reputation, Dodge City appeared to be very peaceful. He entered the saloon and looked around to get his bearings.

"Hello," the man in black said to the lady sitting alone at a corner table. She was casually shuffling a deck of cards, while keeping an eye on the crowd … she was obviously in charge and knew exactly what was happening in every corner of the saloon. "My name's Paladin."

"Howdy, stranger," she responded, momentarily looking at the man dressed in black before turning her attention back to a poker game underway at a nearby table. "My name's Miss Kitty. What brings you to the Long Branch?"

When her gaze returned to the stranger standing between her and the entrance from which he had entered, she took particular notice of his six shooter resting in a black leather holster with a shiny chess knight symbol on its side. It had the look of a tool easily accessible to a man who knew how to use it.

"Nice place you have here," he said. "Nice and quiet. Seems very much like a place that attracts customers having many varied pursuits. Some not so peaceful."

"I like to think we serve all," Miss Kitty responded. "Make yourself at home. Or state your business and get on with it. I'm rather short on time to waste palavering about our patrons."

The man in black looked around and sized up the four men sitting around the nearby table, who were concentrating on the next card to be dealt. "I like to think I can protect the peacefulness of your establishment. Take those gents playing poker. That fella in the green vest seems a mite perturbed about the way cards are being dealt. He's likely to raise a ruckus and call out the dealer for 'mishandling' the cards. Not a good situation for the Long Branch."

Miss Kitty quietly responded, "You're right, but do you see that tall man at the bar talking with Sam, the bartender? His name's Matt Dillon and he's the sheriff here. With Dillon around, I'm not expecting any trouble. No one wants to tangle with him ... including that fella with the green vest."

"Matt Dillon ... I've heard of him," Paladin said. "Seems he has a reputation for no-nonsense law enforcement. I guess you do have things under control ... and since I'm not needed, I reckon I'll just mosey over to the bar and enjoy a drink. Glad to have met you, Miss Kitty."

As he wandered over to an empty stool near the sheriff, he heard Miss Kitty yell out, "Hey, Sam. Give the man in black a whiskey ... on the house."

Paladin smiled and calmly accepted Sam's serving. "Thanks, Sam. Greatly appreciated!"

Just then, an increasingly loud commotion interfered

with his attention to the whiskey in front of him. It was coming from the table of poker players, and the man in the green vest stood and accused the dealer sitting across from him of cheating.

Before Paladin had completely turn around to see what was happening, Dillon had swung into action and whacked the gambler making the ruckus over the head with his pistol … and a sudden quiet befell the room.

"I guess Miss Kitty was right. He wasn't going to be a problem," Paladin thought as Dillon marched the groggy one out the door.

"Sam, I don't think you'll need me as long as Matt Dillon is sheriff here, but just in case, here's my card. Send for me if there's anything I can do to help." With that, the man in black finished his drink and walked out of the Long Branch.

Paladin's next destination was Big Whiskey, Wyoming, where he had been asked to settle a score with a drunk cowboy who had cut up the face of a local prostitute. The whore house had banded together to accumulate enough money to hire a gun fighter to exact revenge on the offending cowboy.

When he arrived, the first thing he did was to check in with the local sheriff where he was told by a deputy, "You're a little late. They already gave the job to a trio of gunmen who completed the task."

"By any chance," asked Paladin, "was one of the gunmen a man named Shane?"

"Nope. It was William Munny and his buddies Ned Logan and the Schofield Kid. Logan was killed in the melee and his body was buried by the townsfolk at the insistence of Munny. He and the Kid wondered off after the deed was done."

"Hmmm," Paladin thought to himself. "A wasted trip." He turned to leave, but asked on the way out, "Where's the sheriff? I'd like to say hello, and offer my services for any other problems he might have."

"Well, you're a little late for him, as well," the deputy replied. "Little Bill and several of his friends were shot deader than a doornail by Munny because they had killed Logan. You might say Munny was a little angry ... but the whole town is better off without that kind of sheriff!"

Looking at the deputy, Paladin said, "I guess you're in for a promotion. Keep me in mind if there's anything I can do to help around here," and he gave the deputy one of his calling cards.

The deputy responded, "I think we're all right for now, but you never know what lies down the road. This is, of course, the wild west."

Paladin thanked him and got on Rafter. "Well, boy. I think we've done our best to be of help. Seems like we're not needed out here. Let's head home." He turned west and set off to cross the Rockies. They had a long ride ahead of them.

_____

Once back in San Francisco, Paladin reverted back to being Joe Starrett, man about town. A few days after returning, he was having drinks in the Hotel Carlton lobby bar with his friends, William Randolph Hearst and Levi Strauss.

He regaled them with his stories of people he encountered on his recent travels through the prairie states, and they listened in rapt attention.

"You know," he concluded, "I was impressed that there were so many individuals out there willing to lend a hand when needed. Everywhere I went there were examples of brave men standing up for justice and the rights of others. This country truly breeds self-reliant and courageous men of good will who insist on the well being of all."

"Your observations are reassuring to me," remarked Hearst. "That's something I'd like to shine a light on in my newspapers."

Joey thought about the progress being made in San Francisco. It was 1887 and Hearst had just assumed management of the San Fransisco Examiner newspaper, and he was making a difference in the lives of people everywhere. The paper had recently been acquired by his father in payment of a gambling debt, and he jumped at the chance to take operational control.

A self-proclaimed populist, Hearst was known for reporting accounts of municipal and financial corruption, often attacking companies in which his own family held an interest. Within a few years, his paper dominated the San Francisco market.

Starrett enjoyed his friendship with Hearst. One of its benefits was being able to converse with so many famous people who worked for or were being interviewed by the Examiner. He particularly enjoyed frequent conversations with Mark Twain and Jack London.

Joey had come a long way from his birthplace in the Wyoming territory.

Sttauss chimed in, "Those men you describe from your travels, Starrett, are also the people who will soon all be wearing the pants I make. Blue jeans are perfectively made for the rigors of western men." His company, the Levi Strauss & Company, was headquartered in San Francisco.

As a result of the sturdiness of the pants he created, the Levi name became synonymous with western wear … and his jeans did become widely accepted as work pants throughout America.

Joey sat back in his chair, took another sip of his drink, and thought to himself, "Even in the cities, there are men demonstrating the American character of bringing civilization and innovation to this brave new world. There's no end to what we in America are capable of with people like this."

———————

Although Paladin wasn't able to assist anyone in trouble on this initial outing, other journeys would establish his reputation for being a man of courage and noble bearing. Much like Shane, he would be a knight in shining armor slaying villains who provoked chaos and embodied evil.

However, Joey did find during his travels what he knew all along would be there ... people of raw courage and righteousness who always seemed to be around to help those who needed their help.

***

Q is for
Quincy

I ask myself … "Why on earth did I pick 'Quincy'? I've never been to a town named 'Quincy' … I've never known anyone named 'Quincy' … I was not even sure how to spell 'Quincy'!" But the word intrigued me.

Perhaps it came to mind because of my early memories of the long-running TV show: 'Quincy M.E.'. Or, maybe from my recollections of celebrities named 'Quincy' … John Quincy Adams, a politician of note … or Quincy Jones, a master of musical notes. Or having heard of towns named 'Quincy' … as in Massachusetts.

So … 'Quincy' it is!

When looking up information about 'Quincy', I learned that it's a boy's name of French origin meaning 'estate of the fifth son'. However, it can also be a girl's name … although there are three times as many boys named Quincy in our country. One website said that 20,785 boys had been named

Quincy since 1880 ... the most in 1977 (715).

With regard to towns named 'Quincy', one source said there are 17 communities in the United States with that name ... 5 in France.

One town ... Quincy, Florida ... was a small community once known as the 'Town of Coca Cola Millionaires' ... the richest town per capita in the US due to early wide-spread investments in Coca Cola securities.

Another town ... Quincy, Pennsylvania ... was known as the place where the phrase 'Kilroy Was Here' originated. It seems that during World War II, James Kilroy – a worker at the Bethlehem Steel Shipyard – chalked the message next to rivets he inspected on ships under construction.

With no time to paint over the markings before the ships went to battle, 'Kilroy Was Here' traveled the globe, where battle-weary GI's adopted the phrase as a rallying cry, scrawling it wherever they went. Soon, the legend sprang up that no matter where the Allied Forces landed, 'Kilroy' somehow managed to get there first. Interesting?

And then there's an animated television series from Japan named 'Bleach' that includes a major race called: 'The Quincy'. It's about a character named Ichigo who has powers obtained from the Grim Reaper and defends humans from evil spirits ... guiding departed souls to the afterlife. Pretty cool, huh?

It seems, The Quincy are a supernatural race largely killed off because they were a threat to humans … the few remaining Quincy survived by disguising themselves as normal civilians. The most powerful Quincy is Yhwach, the leader of The Quincy, who led them during the 'Thousand Year Blood War'.

It's amazing what you find out about even the most quirky of words. Probably the most intriguing reference I found concerned a town named Quincy, Oklahoma, which could not be found on any US maps or modern listings of towns in the state … but it was thought to have been located in Cleveland County. Although searches failed to determine where it was located, rumors persisted of its existence.

This obscure reference of course had to be explored and I do so in my story: 'The Man From Quincy, Oklahoma'.

But, first … I have two 101 word tales for this chapter. I really enjoyed using this story telling form in the last chapter and decided to try my hand at it again.

***

Quincy AKA Jim

My name is Jim, but it wasn't always. I was named Quincy at birth by my folks who thought it was unique and distinguished. As a teenager, however, I didn't want to be unique or distinguished … I simply wanted to fit in.

So, toward the end of my turbulent teen years, I finally convinced my parents that a name-change was the cure-all for a better life. I became Jim … legally.

Whether true or not, I am happier. Now, married and a father, life is good.

I'm very proud of my exceptional son: Quentin … my pride and joy.

***

Birthday Malaise

I have a good friend named Quincy. He was 14 when we met ... and now he's 80.

At his birthday party, we enjoyed grape punch, cheese balls and cake. However, the candles on the cake were many ... too many for Quincy to blow out ... although, he tried.

After three attempts, he gave up, and I helped. We clapped and laughed and had a great time. But the joy was muted in the empty room.

"We've simply lived too long," I mused. "All our friends and family are gone!"

"Alas," Quincy sighed. "Birthday's are just unhappy reminders of better times."

***

The Man From Quincy, Oklahoma

I met a man at the grocery store the other day. It was Saturday morning and I was on one of my 'honey-do' errands. Our paths intersected as we both evaluated the store's selection of apples. He seemed to be looking at me thoughtfully ... his attention was somewhat unnerving ... and after several moments, he said, "My name is Joe." He then slowly glanced away, as if shyly gathering his thoughts for another revelation ... and then said, "I'm from Quincy, Oklahoma."

I smiled and replied, "Hello. I'm Jim. Nice apples, huh?" He said nothing more. After I picked three blemish-free Fuji apples, he also randomly bagged three apples that appeared OK, and followed me as I walked toward the checkout. In line, we quietly waited while my few things were rung up. As I was preparing to leave, I turned to Joe, and smiled, "You have a good day."

His response was a quizzical look that prompted me to ask, "Do I know you?"

"I don't know," he said slowly, and continued pleadingly, "Do I look familiar?" And then strangely repeated, "I'm from Quincy, Oklahoma."

As a native Oklahoma boy, I thought I knew all there was to know about my home state ... but I had never heard of Quincy. I thought, "Maybe he's confused and he's thinking of Quincy, Illinois, or Massachusetts."

His confused state reminded me of my Uncle Harry who had suffered through 8 years of disorientation with Alzheimer's. That recognition immediately caused me to sympathize with Joe, and I turned back and told the cashier, "I'll pay for this man's apples," and handed her the needed cash.

We walked out of the store together. Joe seemed relieved to have me lead the way, and once outside, I asked, "Joe, would you like me to drive you home?" As he mumbled something about not being sure where he lived, I asked, "Do you have someone I could call … or any idea in which direction you live?"

He obviously was having trouble finding an answer, and I recalled the time Uncle Harry had gone missing for two days during his later years. We found out, once he was home, that he had simply not been able to remember where he lived, and he wandered around till he was found by a good Samaritan who took the time to help him get home.

When we tried to reward the good Samaritan in some way, he refused and simply said, "Just be on the lookout for a future encounter who could benefit from an equal measure of kindness. Pay it forward!" This was obviously my chance to render an equal measure of consideration to Joe, who was clearly in need of a friend.

Joe was a man who looked to be in his fifties, and was well dressed and clean shaven … he did not appear to be a derelict. I took Joe by the arm and said, "Let's you and me take a ride and I'll introduce you to my wife, Debra, and our two kids. You can relax in our home while we contact someone who can help you find your way. I'm sure Debra will have lunch ready, and you'll enjoy meeting my family." Joe grinned broadly, as he rode quietly, sitting stiffly, next to me in my Chevy.

As promised, Debra and the kids had just pulled together all the fixings for sandwiches … our timing was perfect as we were greeted with enthusiasm. I introduced Joe to the family. "Joe, this is my wife Debra … and our son, Jerry … and our grown up little girl, Jenny. Guys, this is Joe. I met him at the store and we sort of hit it off. He needs our help finding his way home, and I thought we could all help him."

Joe smiled broadly throughout the introductions just as he had since we first met. As he shook hands with each of the family in turn, he repeated, "Hi. I'm from Quincy, Oklahoma."

During lunch, we chatted aimlessly about our recent experiences, but Joe, though smiling and attentive throughout, was quiet. I tried to draw him into the conversation by telling him about our kids. "Jerry is a budding artist and writer. He has developed a style in both that is truly unique and he's quickly becoming a true talent ... way beyond his 15 years. I'm sure, if pressed, he will be glad to show you some of his work." Joe simply smiled at Jerry, seemingly in appreciation of his abilities.

"And while Jenny is only 12," I continued, "she's already a computer wiz. She's our go-to gal when we have internet questions or need help with our laptops. And she actually outplays all the kids in the neighborhood when it comes to the more competitive games ... she's known in the area as the 'Gamer Shamer', since she puts all of us to shame."

That afternoon, Debra and I made dozens of phone calls to city agencies, medical facilities, religious organizations ... to anyone who might help Joe find his way. Somewhere out there he had a home ... with people who cared about him and were concerned that he had not returned. But by the end of the day, after describing Joe's situation numerous times, the only recommendation given was to make him comfortable and they would get back to us when they had something solid to report.

While we were searching for answers to Joe's situation, he sat at the kitchen table watching Jerry do one of his unique drawings. He said nothing, but clearly enjoyed watching Jerry draw.

Later he went into Jenny's room where she sat at her computer transfixed by the rapidly changing scenario on her screen. When she noticed Joe standing behind her, she said, "See that character?" pointing to a strangely attired girl. "That's Mei and she's my avatar … my identity … in this game called Overwatch. It's one of my favorite games."

Joe looked puzzled, but continued to watch as 'Mei' ran across the screen, blasting away at other strange characters as they came into view. Jenny explained, "Mei has several weather-altering devices that protect her and slow down her opponents, and her Endothermic Blaster shoots icicles and frost streams at her enemies. And this is really neat … she can Cryo-Freeze herself to guard against counterattacks, or obstruct the opposing team's movements with an Ice Wall. I'm at the highest endorsement level … level 5 … and my friends and I are unstoppable! Even the guys playing the game say so."

While Joe was spending time with Jerry and Jenny, Debra and I waited for a call that would enable us to help him get home. "Jim," Debra said, "you should take a picture of Joe while we're all sitting around this afternoon. We can use that when we talk to people about finding Joe's home." When we were all together again, I did as Debra suggested and took pictures of the family … focusing on Joe.

As evening approached, and no call was received, I turned to Debra and said, "It looks like we should set up a bed in the den for Joe. There's nothing more we can do tonight. At least we can make him comfortable and let him get a good night's sleep, and we'll tackle his predicament again tomorrow."

After dinner, we watched a little TV as a family and chatted about whatever came to mind … but Joe simply sat quietly erect and didn't contribute to the conversation … even when invited to say something. Although he did say again … several times … "I'm from Quincy, Oklahoma." Even though quiet and content to not contribute, Joe seemed to have settled in … happy to be a 'member' of our family.

The next morning, we all gathered in the kitchen for breakfast, but Joe did not appear. I knocked on the door to the den, and when there was no answer, I entered and, much to my surprise, found the bed made and Joe gone.

"He's not here," I said as I returned to the kitchen. "The only thing remaining is a 1885 Morgan silver dollar plopped on a made-up bed wrapped in a note that simply says: 'Sunday in Quincy'. Did anyone see him leave, or hear anything?"

After confirming he was not inside our home, we went outside and looked around the neighborhood for our missing guest. But we returned disappointed and called the authorities. "Yes … he's missing. No … I don't know where he might go or anything about him. As I said when we talked yesterday, he seems to be a victim of Alzheimer's and he was unable to tell us anything that might help him get home."

Our conversations with various agencies were disappointing, and we decided that there was nothing more we could do. They would be on the lookout for Joe and, once found, get him the help he needed.

While our role in Joe's life had been brief, we all sat around the kitchen table reminiscing about the few hours we had known him ... even though we knew very little about our silent guest, his smiling demeanor and his interest in our conversations had endeared him to each of us. Now we all sat silently at the table remembering this gentle man named Joe.

"All right, guys ... surely, we must know something about Joe that will help find him," I said finally. "What clues did he leave behind? And what do you suppose his note ... 'Sunday in Quincy' ... means?"

We each thought back, but the only thing we knew about Joe was that he was from Quincy, Oklahoma. He had reminded us of that several times. "Okay ... Jenny, can you search the Internet and find out where Quincy, Oklahoma, is and how far it is from here. I'm sure it can't be too far ... we're pretty centrally located here in Oklahoma City."

I turned and looked at Jerry, "And Jerry, can you create a poster asking anyone who knows or sees Joe to give us a call. You can use one of the photos we took of him last night. Be sure and stress that he may seem disoriented and in need of help."

I took Debra's hand and said, "Debra, you and I can help post the flyers around the neighborhood and wherever he might go … and maybe talk with the local radio station to issue a public service announcement about Joe needing help. He's got to be around here somewhere!"

Later that morning, when we had finished our tasks and the flyers had been posted, we reassembled in the living room. We were all weary and disappointed that we seemed to have done all we could … and had not located Joe. Jenny, usually the quiet one, talked rapidly about what she had discovered on line.

"With regard to a town named Quincy," she said, "there is no town with that name currently located in Oklahoma. The only reference to Quincy in Oklahoma is to a community in Cleveland County that is rumored to have had that name, but it's not on any maps or listings of present towns. Not much to go on, huh?"

"Clearly not much," I commented. "We've got to think of other ways of finding out who Joe is and where we might find him."

"Well," spoke up Debra, "Quincy, Oklahoma, was clearly important to him, since he mentioned coming from there several times. And his note did say 'Sunday in Quincy' … and today is Sunday. Why don't we take a road trip to Cleveland County and see what we can learn about our mysterious town, and its native son. It would, in any case, be a fun day trip. Jenny … print out what we know about Quincy, Oklahoma, and we'll leave and get lunch on the road."

As we were getting ready to leave, I received a call from Bill Davis, a friend at our local hospital with whom I had talked earlier about Joe. "Jim … I'm returning your call about the man you encountered with a befuddled attitude. We've had something come up I think you'll find interesting. Our hospital has had inquiries recently from affiliated hospitals that involved similar stories.

"One call involved a man found wandering around a flea market on the outskirts of Enid. He was aided and treated to a meal by a young lady named Beth, but she eventually took him to a homeless shelter when he couldn't remember where he lived. He kept repeating that he was from Quincy, Oklahoma … just like the fella you told me about.

"And then there was another report about a man aimlessly wandering the streets in downtown Tulsa who kept telling everyone who passed by that his name was Joe and he was from … you guessed it … Quincy, Oklahoma. He was aided by an older couple who went out of their way to help him and eventually took him to and paid for a room at a local Fairfield Inn when authorities couldn't determine where he was from.

"It sounds like these two reports involved the same guy you found. The interesting thing is that both of these men disappeared from their overnight lodgings, and no one knows where they went. And each of the benefactors received a silver dollar from Joe, wrapped in a note saying something about Quincy and Sunday. This was odd enough that I thought I'd check with you about your Joe. Any similarity?"

When I had a moment to think about these coincidences, I responded, "Very similar. In fact, our Joe also disappeared and the only thing we found this morning was an 1885 Morgan silver dollar on the bed he had been provided, with a note reading 'Sunday in Quincy'. Creepy!"

After I had thanked Bill for the update and hung up, I relayed what he had told me to the family. "It seems the mystery of our guy named Joe has become a little more complex."

Debra quietly turned and said, "Well, there've been other reports as well." She unfolded the morning paper to an inside page with an article titled 'The Man From Quincy'. "Apparently, similar stories have been reported from other towns in Oklahoma as well … nine sightings over the past week.

"I know, I know, she said exasperatedly. "With what Bill reported, and our experience, Joe seems to have appeared at least 9, maybe 12, times in 7 days in different parts of the state … and who knows how many other sightings were unreported.

"And they all share three common elements:

he's a quiet guy named Joe … he's from Quincy, Oklahoma … and he leaves behind a silver dollar and a note. Can Joe be in so many places in seven days? That certainly adds to the mystery. What's going on here?"

"I don't know. But let's get in the car," I responded, "and see what we can find in Cleveland County."

A short time later, we arrived in Norman, the largest city in Cleveland County. "Well, assuming there was once a Quincy in this county," I offered, "it's probably been absorbed by a larger town … like Norman. Let's keep our eyes open as I drive around the suburbs for something referring to Quincy."

It wasn't five minutes later that we came upon a run down bowling alley still attracting a crowd judging from the number of cars in the parking lot … and its name was 'Quincy Bowl'. We parked and smiled at our success … this was indeed akin to finding a needle in a haystack. We jumped out to see what we might find inside.

Inside, we looked around and saw a group of 20 or so people congregating in the lounge … they seemed to be the only patrons … and they weren't bowling. As we approached, we overheard "Joe" mentioned several times … and "he was from Quincy, Oklahoma" in response to someone's question.

This piqued our curiosity, and we tapped one of the participants on the shoulder and asked, "Hi …

my name's Jim and this is my family. What's going on here? Do you folks know Joe from Quincy, Oklahoma?"

The man turned, smiled and responded, "Hi. My name's George, and I'm not sure what's going on … but, we're all here trying to resolve a mystery that's touched each of us. We've all had the same experience … we've each been approached by a stranger who seemed to be lost and we offered our help. The name of the stranger is always 'Joe' and he's from …… "

"I know," I interrupted, holding out the silver dollar Joe left behind, "he's from Quincy, Oklahoma. And, I'll bet, he mysteriously disappeared during the night leaving his benefactor a silver dollar and a note saying 'Sunday in Quincy'."

"Ahhh, I see you've had the same experience," he said with a grin, holding out a similar silver dollar. "Well, each of us has journeyed here from various towns in Oklahoma in search of answers. But we've only stumbled upon an even greater mystery: are we all meant to be here … at the Quincy Bowl … on this day … for some reason? What has prompted us to make this journey and what do we do now that we're all together?"

I glanced over at Debra and our kids as they looked quizzically at me. "That's a very good question. Has anyone come up with any ideas that make sense?"

Just then, the lights in the lounge flickered and

dimmed. The group went eerily quiet, and we all looked around as if the cause might be obviously discernible. Accepting this as just another facet of the mystery of 'Joe', we each turned to the person next to us and resumed our conversations … albeit much more quietly. Then, all of a sudden, the dim lights in the lounge shut off entirely and we were doused in total darkness.

I reached out for Debra and the kids, and we huddled in our little family circle … sensing that remaining quiet was advisable. Not a sound was uttered by others in the lounge … the quiet was, as they say, deafening.

Just as suddenly, the lights came on and we all blinked rapidly … trying to acclimatize our eyes to the harsh brightness now bathing the lounge. Then we noticed everyone was turning toward the counter on one side of the lounge. There, sitting quietly sipping a soda, was Joe … the mystery man from Quincy, Oklahoma, who, by disappearing, had brought us all together.

Joe, setting down his soda, slowly spun around on his counter stool and faced the group. Looking at each of us in turn, he began speaking. "As an obviously confused and needy stranger, I wandered in towns throughout Oklahoma. Without pleading for help, you … and in some cases, your families … are the only ones who … voluntarily … offered me comfort and support without reservation.

"And even when you found I had departed without notice, you felt obligated to be sure I was safely home. You surmised my note ... 'Sunday in Quincy' ... might be a clue as to where I could be found. You took the time to find me and you did this with negligible information on which to rely. Other than my first name, you only knew I was from Quincy, Oklahoma ... a town that doesn't exist on today's maps. And you ended up here on the day mentioned in my note ... some traveling great distances."

Suddenly, one of the men in our group, spoke up and asked, "I'm assuming you don't really need our help. But, can you tell us a little bit about who you are and why we're here?"

"As to who I am ... I know you're all curious ... but it really doesn't matter. I'm just a guy named Joe. But this gathering is not about me ... it's about you! You are the ones who came to my aid and provided what I was seeking ... confirmation that there are people who would provide help to a distressed stranger in his time of need. You are too few, but you demonstrated by action that the spark of compassion and humanity still exists in today's world.

"I wanted you all here to thank you for being who you are ... for you to see that you're not alone ... and to let others know that good deeds are recognized and appreciated. Just remember, kindness is contagious ... so, please, keep up the good deeds!"

With that, Joe slipped off his stool and began

strolling toward the front door … when suddenly he stopped and once again faced the group. "You know," he said, "with all the publicity surrounding the appearance, disappearance and reappearance of 'Joe from Quincy, Oklahoma', I expect you will receive a lot of media attention. Be sure and let them know that I really appreciate the compassion and kindness you showed me!"

He turned and continued his stroll, when he again stopped. Looking at us, he said, "By the way, those silver dollars I left you at my departure are Morgan's and they are one of the most popular coins in the US Mint's history … and 1885 was a very low mintage year for Morgan silver dollars … which means they are valued at considerably more than a dollar." And then he was gone.

Some of us ran to the front door, but as we exited the building, Joe was nowhere in sight. It was evening by this time, and he had once again vanished into the night.

To this day, folks in Oklahoma talk about Joe from Quincy, Oklahoma … about the mystery of his wandering in towns throughout Oklahoma … and of his message regarding the worthiness of showing more humanity to those in need.

As to the 1885 Morgan silver dollars, it's rumored that one of Joe's benefactors sold his coin to a collector for more than a million dollars.

***

R is for

Recluse

As my years accumulate, I value time with family and friends more ardently than ever, and I look at those who choose a more solitary life with curiosity. When I came upon the word 'recluse' while looking at words for my 'R' chapter, I decided that the curiosity of such a solitary lifestyle ... usually chosen voluntarily ... could be useful in developing stories for this book. So ... that's the focus for the next few pages.

> *So, what do Emile Dickinson (poet), Stanley Kubrick (film director), Bobby Fischer (chess champion), and Nikola Tesla (inventor, engineer, and physicist) have in common? Of course, they were all considered very successful in their fields ... but they were also each considered examples of a recluse in their day.*

I think it's interesting that someone would prefer isolation in lieu of being in the company of others

… a recluse carries that to its extreme. Now, I do understand that occasionally time to oneself can be therapeutic and refreshing, but … a true recluse finds that state of 'alone' time as a necessity for his (or her) wellbeing, for many different reasons.

First of all, you need to understand that for a recluse, it's not always a reaction to an inability to socialize, a fear of contamination, or a need to focus on personal endeavors. It's more often a matter of attaining a level of comfort with oneself and having the means of providing for one's isolation.

> *Other people who demonstrated reclusive behavior include: Greta Garbo (actress) Howard Hughes (aviator, businessman), Harper Lee (novelist) and Edvard Munch (painter).*

As for me, I am not a recluse, but I admit to a real fascination with those who are. Thus, I'm ready to begin my 'R' chapter. But, if I'm to write about a recluse, I should have a back-story on why my hero chose to isolate himself.

Should my recluse suffer from a psychological malady, such as a post traumatic stress disorder, social anxiety disorder, apathy, autism, depression, obsessive-compulsive disorder, intellectual disability, schizoid personality disorder, schizotypal personality disorder or avoidant personality disorder? Does he isolate himself for religious reasons, to practice self-sufficiency, in hiding for some criminal activity, or due to an unrequited love? So many reasons … it's a wonder more of us have not become reclusive.

But I think I'll start off with a story about a man … a true recluse … who lived near our daughter's lake house and was the subject of much neighborly gossip.

> *Then there's the use of the word in the world of insects that expands possible story lines that would evoke fear and dread in virtually all of us … the deadly 'Brown Recluse' spider who likes to hide out in dark old boots or undisturbed corners of a basement.*

***

The Recluse of Kerr Lake

Jerry died yesterday!

Not many people noticed or will miss his presence. But, as a subject for local gossips, his passing will make their chatter less interesting. He was what can be called a recluse: away from his home only occasionally … preferring to live apart from others … scurrying past people in passing … avoiding eye contact when approached.

Jerry lived in a community on the shore of Kerr Lake in North Carolina. Our daughter, Mary Anne, and her family also had a 'get-away' home in that area, which is how we became acquainted with Jerry. We enjoyed many lake activities and relaxing hours there. More importantly, it gave us invaluable time with our twin grandsons … and their parents … as well as to hear the latest gossip on Jerry, the local recluse.

Our daughter's home was located in a wooded area on the western shoreline and had been upgraded over the years with loving do-it-yourself projects. They had refurbished or replaced every aspect, from flooring to plumbing and wall/window treatments … every surface, inside and outside, had been freshly painted … even the surrounding natural landscaping and dock had been enhanced. They had clearly made the original rundown house into a comfortable and beautiful home.

While their home was located on more than an acre

of land, there were other homes in the surrounding area ... some with year-around residents and others owned by 'fair weather' families like our daughter's.

We often sat around on their shady deck listening to tales told of lives lived and memories remembered. Conversations often turned to the latest sightings of Jerry. It seems he was a 'loner' and the subject of much curiosity and speculation. We wondered what he did in his isolation ... why he preferred his own company more than socializing with others ... and what caused him to become reclusive.

Apparently, Jerry had arrived in the area 40 or so years ago following the death of his parents in an auto accident. He had inherited their lake house which was within an easy walk of our daughter's home.

His home is a one-level house finished with wood and stone situated on over an acre of wooded property. Since his arrival, he had erected a five foot high wood privacy fence around much of his property ... very unusual in this community of residents that prided themselves on their love of open space. A sign at the entrance to his property identified his home as 'The Refuge' ... very appropriate for a recluse.

It was said that Jerry was younger than me ... in his 60's... but he looked to be considerably older. He was a recognizable figure in the community ... typically clad in blue jeans and a navy sweat shirt ...

even on hot and humid days … with whiskers several days old, and shaggy hair. When he was seen outside 'The Refuge', he walked slowly … taking small, deliberate steps … as if fearful of losing his footing.

There were many stories that the locals told of Jerry … some of them may have even been true. I overheard one conversation while visiting the Clarksville library between Janet, the librarian, and Rachel, the town gossip.

"Did you hear," Rachel was saying, "Jerry was seen roaming the streets early this morning before all the shops had opened. He seemed to be talking to himself and looking through every trash can along the walkway. Now why would he be doing that? Seems mighty suspicious to me!"

"Rachel … where did you hear that?" Janet responded. "That doesn't sound in the least bit like Jerry. He's a loner, but he's not a looney."

Rachel hesitated, but quickly blurted out, "Well, he's always been a bit mysterious! How much do we really know about him? He keeps to himself and … does he really have any friends? I don't think so. And remember that time he was seen digging up something in his yard? His neighbors spotted him over that fence of his and said he kept digging in that one spot for several days. What do you suppose he was trying to bury?"

With that, Janet turned to help a customer who had

a book to check out, and Rachel wandered away. It didn't look like Rachel had been convincing in spreading a new rumor about Jerry ... at least to Janet.

The tale of Jerry digging in his yard was well known in the community, and there were many explanations given to what he was doing, but no one knew for sure. The particular plot he was working on could not be clearly seen over the fence, but that didn't stop the locals from speculating as to what he was up to.

Peter, his neighbor on the west, seemed to be well informed. "He's clearing the spot," he said, "to create a foundation for a new patio with a barbecue grill to entertain guests." Of course, Jerry never invited guests into his compound, so a place to entertain seemed unlikely.

His eastern neighbors, Grace and Ned, thought he was simply cultivating an area to plant a garden. "He's decided," Grace said, "that by growing some of his own vegetables, he wouldn't have to go into town as often." That certainly sounded plausible.

But some of the more ludicrous suggestions about Jerry's activities included: "he's burying a body", "he's building a bomb shelter", "he's creating a landing pad for alien visitors," ... and on and on. It's as if the town was addicted to rumors of Jerry's reclusiveness ... a favorite topic of conversation.

I chuckled to myself as speculation about Jerry

became more fanciful … and more implausible. I preferred to think he was simply working the soil to beautify his property and get a little exercise.

Curiosity about Jerry was very much the community's obsession. When in the area, people would intentionally stroll past his property so they could peer over his fence in hopes of seeing what Jerry was up to. Sightings would then be passed along during conversations with others … and hence Jerry's reputation as the community's recluse grew wildly.

I'd never met Jerry, but the one story about him that seemed most rational revolved around his arrival here. Janet, our local librarian and amateur genealogist, had apparently taken an interest in Jerry and explored as best she could his history.

"Jerry had been a Marine as a young man," she said, "and returned from his final tour in Vietnam in 1975 severely traumatized. I've been told by a good friend at the Library of Congress that Jerry had been on the last helicopter leaving Saigon during the evacuation of the US Embassy. He'd received several awards for military valor and for wounds suffered in action there … but Jerry never talked about them.

"He was honorably discharged in San Diego," she continued, "and at about the same time received word that both of his parents were killed in an auto accident. Needless to say, his return to civilian life was an emotional nightmare … having to contend with the traumatic stress experienced in Vietnam and the loss of the only family he had ever known."

Janet smiled as she continued. "It was during this period that he arrived in our community and took up residence in the home on Kerr Lake his parents had left him." Janet had obviously grown to discount all the strangeness attributed to Jerry ... and even seemed to admire Jerry.

But the strange events attributed to Jerry persisted over time and his reputation reflected those oddities. Many times, conversations included the phrase, "He's an odd duck."

I remember one time, at a gathering at our daughter's home, one of the guests ... I think it was Richard ... told of the time Jerry was seen marching around his property in his Marine dress uniform. "He had a rifle slung over his shoulder," he confided seriously, "and had a very serious look. I think he's finally lost it, and he's preparing to rejoin his old unit for an armed attack on an imaginary enemy."

That caused many to ask the local sheriff to "lock him up before he shoots someone in the neighborhood." Of course, when the sheriff checked on Jerry, there was nothing that could substantiate their fears ... or even that Jerry still had his uniform.

On another occasion, Betsy, the owner of our local bakery, repeated a really weird sighting. "I heard it on good authority that Jerry was seen in town on a shopping trip and one of the things he bought was a pink umbrella. He walked all the way to his home with that umbrella tucked under his arm. What on earth would he want a pink umbrella for? He's clearly out of his mind. There's not even a hint of rain in the forecast."

Well, a while later, Janet reported that Amy, her 8 year old granddaughter had anonymously received a pink umbrella for her birthday. "I just know it was Jerry who remembered Amy's birthday. They had talked quietly one day when he had met her in the library."

It's amazing when you stop to think about it. All Jerry wanted to do was to live his life in solitude and yet it caused his neighbors to imagine so many strange tales about him … each more far fetched than the last. It was with his passing, however, that the community heard the one story that had not been told while he lived.

Of course, it was Janet who told all who would listen about his last days in Vietnam. "You, of course, know about the loss of his parents in that tragic auto accident and its deep affect on him as a young man. But, just prior to that, Jerry was also involved as a Marine in the Vietnam War and all the pressures that entailed.

"He was in Saigon during the traumatic winding down of America's withdrawal and was subjected to the desperation of the retreating US Forces and imperiled South Vietnamese people. In fact, he drove a bus around on April 29, 1975, to collect the few remaining Americans and deliver them to the US embassy … the day before the final evacuation.

"He made several trips through the chaotic streets of Saigon where he encountered desperate Vietnamese fearful of the American withdrawal and the arrival of North Vietnamese troops who would not be sympathetic to the locals who had supported the US effort. Panic was spreading everywhere.

"Jerry did an extraordinary job getting those who needed to be transported to the embassy. But, everywhere he went, there were terrified Vietnamese screaming "Cúu tôi! … Cúu tôi!" ("Save me! Save me!"), but he had to drive past them to safely deliver only those who were authorized.

"There were many scenes of women with wailing babies pleading to be taken … of men in halting English screaming "I help Americans … you help me!" He knew that many of those he ignored would not survive the communist retaliation."

Janet, at this point, would often stop her narrative and look around at her audience who were listening intently and feeling the horror and pain Jerry must have been experiencing.

She continued, "Once he completed his roundup, he spent a fretful night sharing guard duty at the embassy to thwart anyone seeking unauthorized entry … force had been exerted to hold the perimeter … resulting in no rest that night.

"The next morning, the assembled group of final evacuees scrambled to the roof, destroying sensitive papers and barricading the stairway as they went. The downstairs perimeter was quickly breached by fearful Vietnamese and the din of their marauding could be heard below as looting commenced ... pleas to be taken to "America" were heart wrenching.

Once on the roof, helicopters were lifting off as many as they could. The ambassador and the flag of the United States of America were on one leaving at 5:00am and the signal went out, "Tiger Out", which confirmed the ambassador's safe exit.

"Jerry and 80 or so of his comrades remaining after the ambassador's departure waited fearfully for the helicopters to return for them, but their return had been delayed. Someone controlling the evacuation flights had misinterpreted the signal "Tiger Out" to mean everyone had been rescued … not just the ambassador. Fear gripped every soldier on the roof as they envisioned being left behind.

"Finally, Sgt. Juan Valdez, the detachment commander on the roof, got through on the radio and helicopters returned for those still there. Jerry was on the last helicopter leaving the roof of the embassy that morning and watched as Sgt. Valdez climbed aboard … the last US serviceman to get on as the chopper lifted off. All eyes on board stared below as they flew over the burning city and realized that the American mission in Vietnam had been an abject failure."

Everyone who heard Janet recount the horror of those final days in Vietnam had a new respect for Jerry and rued not being able to know him better. And now, Jerry was gone.

Strangely, all those who talked endlessly about Jerry's unconventional life ... the local recluse ... now remembered fondly this quiet man. Jerry had suddenly become a respected member of the Lake Kerr community ... who had proudly served as a Marine of heroic stature and became one of their own.

As for his passing ... it is said he died of natural causes in his sleep ... alone as he preferred. Janet believed he died smiling ... with visions of his parents once again at his side.

The local recluse had finally found peace.

***

The Reluctant Recluse

The Arrival

Jack smiled as he stepped off the plane onto the tarmac at the small airport in Marquette, Michigan. It was early March, 1992, and icy winds swirled around as he and George Maxwell briskly walked toward the nearly empty one-room terminal.

He wrapped his coat tightly around his body and raised its collar hoping to protect himself from the foul weather. But, even in early afternoon, his heavy coat offered little protection from the coldness of the warmest part of the day.

Once inside, he turned to George, his 'handler' from the US Marshall's office, and asked, "Where in the hell are we ... Siberia? Couldn't you find a more hospitable place for me to start my new life? March 9th will henceforth be known as the day Jack Evans arrived in nowheresville."

George chuckled and replied, "Just learn to live with it. You're lucky to be alive and in the witness protection program. Think of this new lease on life as your reward for being a prime witness for the prosecution of John Gotti ... your testimony will help get that scumbag convicted."

Jack had been an unintentional eye witness to Gotti when he shot Louie Castelano in cold blood at a New York diner. He had ducked behind the counter after the shooting just as Gotti turned in his direction and had only been saved when Gotti ran out of the diner ... panicked by the sound of sirens approaching the murder scene. While he had not wanted to testify, Jack did the right thing even though he would have to start a new life to avoid retaliation ... he entered the witness protection program.

They proceeded to a waiting car and drove leisurely to a suburb on the north side of Marquette called Lakeview. It was situated along the shore of Lake Superior and was clearly populated by commuters working in the 'big city' of Marquette. While it had a variety of stores along Main Street offering all the conveniences nearby residents needed, a 'New York City' it was not!

They stopped in front of the Woolworth 'Five and Dime' Store. "Come on," George said. "Let's get you settled in your new residence." He led Jack to a street-side door next to Woolworth's. They entered and walked up a flight of dimly lit stairs and along a hallway above the 'five and dime' leading to Apartment #13. "This is it ... your hide-a-way."

Jack entered and looked around at the sparsely furnished living room-dining room-kitchen ... a separate bedroom was off to the left of the entrance. Obviously, the owner had not spent a great deal on decor, and the previous tenants had worn away any semblance of charm.

"Well, anyone looking for me will never think of looking for me here," Jack said sarcastically. "I'm beginning to see your method of keeping me safe."

George gave Jack the key, and turned to leave. "There's a folder on the table there giving you some information on your new life and what you can and cannot do. Read it carefully and keep your head down. I'll check in occasionally to see how you're doing. Until then … have fun!"

As George closed the door behind him, Jack was left alone … a new beginning. Jack was now officially a 'nobody'.

For the next several days, Jack isolated himself in the apartment and read and reread all the material George had left for him. The old analog TV in the room didn't work, so he listened a lot to the radio. He nibbled on items of food left for him, dreaming of lunches of corned beef on rye … his favorite food. In his old life, he ate at the Carnegie's Deli on 7th Avenue in Midtown Manhattan at least weekly.

The essence of his instructions amounted to becoming a virtual recluse … a recluse in the reclusive community of Lakeview, Michigan. He was told to not leave the area, contact any relatives or friends, or do anything that would increase his visibility. His new name was Jack Walters, and if asked he would say he came to Marquette from

Los Angeles to do some fishing and get over a bad breakup with his long time girl friend.

A bank account had been set up in his name and $500 would be deposited each month into the account for one year. After a year, the payments would stop and he would be expected to have a job and provide his own source of income.

The Apartment

As Jack became more resigned to his situation, he looked around his apartment and decided he had to make some changes. First of all, it needed a thorough cleaning and he took the time to scrub down kitchen surfaces, dust tables and cabinets, and sweep the floors ... chores he hadn't done in decades.

He removed the few clothes he brought from his suitcases and put them away in the bedroom. With that, he smiled as he once again looked around at his now more pleasant abode.

Jack also made a list of things he needed to purchase. "I need to use some of that money they're giving me to get food and other supplies," he thought. "Not much money, but I can stretch it out and buy stuff over time." He smiled again as he thought, "This is a far cry from my life as a New York accountant."

When he was feeling particularly bored one day, he decided to explore his building. He wandered down the hallway and counted 5 other apartments on his floor. There was also a third floor with 6 more apartments, and a stairway leading up to the roof where a patio-like platform overlooking Lake Superior was located.

The one bright spot … he met his next door neighbor, nearly running into her as he was returning to his apartment. She was somewhat younger than Jack, but her twinkling blue eyes and big smile gave him hope that life in Lakeview would be easier to take than he had feared.

"Hello," he blurted out. "My name's Jack … I'm in #13. I'm sorry I almost knocked you over … I'm new here and wasn't paying attention to where I was going." He hesitated, and finally said nervously, "We've got a real palatial residence here, with our very own 'five and dime' down below."

Her smile grew larger as she replied, "It's not so bad once you get settled. You'll see. My name's Alice, and I've been here long enough to be somewhat familiar with all the places to see and be seen if you need any help."

"Thanks," he said. "I look forward to having your help." With that, he turned, mumbled a goodbye and went on to his apartment, thinking "What's the matter with me. That was the most adolescent conversation I've had since I was a teenager."

The Town

One afternoon, when it was not quite as cold as when he first arrived, he decided to explore the area. He had asked Alice where he should go and she offered to be his "official guide" if he wanted ... he accepted, without hesitation.

He put on his coat and Alice led him around Lakeview, pointing out the main sights and where he could find this and that. After strolling for the better part of the afternoon, they went to the Marquette Diner and had a half-way decent meal. He learned that she was a long-time single mom from Detroit and had always loved Lake Superior. So when her daughter left for college, she decided to migrate to Marquette, where she found Lakeview.

Jack commented as they were having a cup of coffee, "Well, our town's not Los Angeles, but I'm beginning to see that it has a charm all of its own.

The city of Marquette, of which Lakeview was just a suburb, had a population of around 20,000 people. It was the largest city in the Upper Peninsula of Michigan. All regions of Marquette were serviced by MarqTran, a public bus system. Alice said, "MarqTran will take you almost anywhere in the city and is both inexpensive and easy to use."

He learned that there were only four options for dining in Lakeview. In addition to the fountain service at Woolworth's, there was the Marquette

Diner two doors down from their apartment, a burger bar opposite the one-screen movie theater, and the 'Laker Seafood and Bar' near the lake. "And none of them had corned beef on their menus," he mused.

With the knowledge Alice gave him on their tour of Lakeview, he spent many afternoons walking around, spending most of his time strolling along Lake Superior. There were several piers and four or five benches along the shore where he often sat watching the few boats sail in and out.

He was intrigued with the little bit of fishing already underway this early in the season. Boats returned each evening from their fishing trips, and he occasionally spoke with crew members when he was having a beer at the 'Laker Bar'. He found out that a 'Laker' was the nickname given to Lake Trout, a widely sought catch by many fishermen in the area.

Employment

Jack was beginning to feel more comfortable in his new life. He knew his way around town and where to go for whatever he needed. He had also met a few people and judged this to be a very friendly town. But, he recognized that he had better find some employment to augment his income and solidify his standing in the community.

Fortunately, his opportunity came as he exited his apartment one day and spotted a sign in the window of the Woolworth store, 'Wanted - Stockroom Supervisor'. He went in and applied for the position, and was immediately hired. He listed his experience in Los Angeles as bookkeeper clerk (as was suggested in the documents on his back story that George had left), and that helped elevate his application ... along with there being no other applicants.

He started his new job the next day, and enjoyed working in the backroom ... perfect for remaining unnoticed. And he liked having something productive to do. The store manager was very helpful in explaining the job requirements and he learned quickly how to be a valued member of the store team.

It also helped him personally as he was able to bank a regular paycheck each week ... watching his available finances grow rather than steadily decline. He now had a net worth exceeding $500 ... hurray!

Corned Beef on Rye

The one aspect of his new life that was still a disappointment was the unavailability of a good corned beef on rye sandwich. He not only couldn't find corned beef on any local menu, but rye bread was not a regular stock item at the local grocery store. Bummer!

He thought to himself, "Well, if I can't get what I want in a restaurant, I'll just have to learn to cook it myself." So he set about finding a recipe for cooking corned beef, brought in the cookware and spices he would need, and ordered a cut of prime beef brisket from the local butcher.

After several tests, he found the particular recipe that resulted in the flavor and tenderness he remembered from New York. Feeling confident, he decided to host Alice for a corned beef and cabbage dinner, being careful to have enough corned beef left for sandwiches on rye the next day.

The dinner was a resounding success. Alice loved it and clearly thought dearly of Jack for having invited her to share his memorable meal. She even came back the next day for corned beef on rye sandwiches.

At about this same time, Jack learned that on April 2nd, John Gotti had been convicted on all charges and would be spending the rest of his life in prison. This was an enormous relief to Jack, although he knew that his life was still in danger as Gotti retained sufficient influence to seek revenge on all those who testified at his trial.

But in spite of his danger, he chuckled when he read that James Fox, of the FBI's New York Field Office, announced at a press conference, "The Teflon is gone. The don is covered with Velcro, and all the charges stuck."

Fighting Depression

By this time, Jack had settled into a solitary routine

as George had suggested. His occasional visits with Alice helped dispel the resulting loneliness, but he generally avoided a wider interaction with the community. He was looked upon as a recluse by others, but he knew this intentional lifestyle was what would keep him unnoticed … and alive.

However, even knowing the importance of distancing himself socially for the time being, he nonetheless suffered an emptiness that began to take its toll. He frequently wondered if living a reclusive life was worth the depression that seemed to result. He even began to question his decision to do the 'right' thing … to testify. Was that really his best option?

His answer was always … "Yes" … but, he had to find some way out of his doldrums. He decided he would get to know Alice better, and let her help bring a bit of cheer into his life.

Romance Blooms

Jack had not had a woman in his life since his wife died 20 years before. It wasn't that he was no longer interested, but his wife, Gloria, was so important to him and her sudden loss was so traumatic that he couldn't find room in his heart for anyone else.

Alice was different. Their friendship grew slowly, and comfortably, without the angst of courtship and conquest interfering. In fact, the casual meeting and easy-going activities together established a feeling of fun and excitement even before they were aware of their romantic attraction.

Jack was always happy when he was with her, and she was always smiling. They found themselves making up excuses for spending time with each other … and times apart seemed less and less enjoyable. Their growing companionship was very satisfying to both … all the right elements for a blossoming romance. It also seemed that neither minded at all the direction their lives were taking.

Alice often pressed him about his prior life, but Jack evaded her questions and stuck to the biography of Jack Walters in the documents provided by George. This storyline was by now feeling contrived, and he rued the day when (and if) he would have to tell her he had been lying to her.

He did, however, tell her how much he enjoyed several trips to New York City, and that he would like to go there with her some day. "That was where I fell in love with corned beef on rye sandwiches … at Carnegie's Deli in Midtown Manhattan."

Warmer Days

By the end of April, the weather in Marquette had begun to get a little warmer. The iciness of his arrival in early March was no longer a factor. This enabled Jack and Alice to enjoy time outdoors and they spent many hours strolling along the shoreline … talking endlessly about every subject imaginable …

except about who Jack Walters really was and why he changed his name from Jack Evans.

They both enjoyed their walks. Jack particularly enjoyed hearing Alice talk about Lake Superior. It always excited her, and he came to understand why she chose to come to Marquette. "Lake Superior," she said, "is the largest lake in the world … by surface area … and it's a fresh water lake fed by over 200 rivers."

It amazed him … the extent of her knowledge about the area. "It's also a very deep lake with an average depth of 483 feet, and it has an unusually low temperature estimated at an average of under 36° Fahrenheit. And, get this … there have been about 350 shipwrecks on the lake with over 10,000 lives lost … and the lake is known to 'never give up the dead' because of the cold water temperature."

Jack interrupted her at this point and said, "I was just reading the other day that the last ship sunk in Lake Superior was the SS Edmund Fitzgerald … an American freighter that sank in a storm on November 10, 1975. The entire crew of 29 was lost. That ship was the largest vessel sailing on the Great Lakes, and the largest to have ever sunk there."

They walked on a little further and Jack turned toward her and said, "Why don't we charter a boat and get a little different perspective of our lake? Maybe even get in a little fishing. I hear the Lake Trout are plentiful this time of year and it would be fun."

Alice agreed and they made arrangements for an all day trip. The captain of the boat promised he would show them all the interesting areas nearby and they would return with enough fish to satisfy their hunger for several days. "Perfect," Alice said.

On the day of the sailing, the captain made good on his promise and they thoroughly enjoyed their tour. He even regaled them with his knowledge of the lake. "We happen to be in one of the better fishing areas on Lake Superior," he said. "We will be going out to Standard Rock which was named the 'loneliest place on the continent'. The locals say it might be the loneliest place, but the fish are definitely not lonely because some of the best fishing in the country is located around this small island.

"It's only a 40 mile trip from Marquette," he continued. "We'll be going there a little late today. The early morning hours are best for catching fish in the shallow waters. When the sun comes up, the fish drop down to the lower reefs making them harder to catch."

Apparently it was early enough in the season that some of the fish stayed obligingly at catchable levels. Jack and Alice each caught several good sized Lake Trout and they returned smiling happily.

'Mr. Fedora' Visits

It was not always quite as uneventful as Jack would have liked. One day, he decided to take a MarqTran bus to explore the further reaches of his refuge. His destination ... downtown Marquette. While on the bus, however, clouds moved in and a heavy downpour dampened his plans to get out and walk around.

While he enjoyed being able to take in the sights from his rolling chariot, he missed being able to stretch his legs and explore close up the many stores in the 'big city'. As they drove along Front Street and passed the Landmark Inn, probably the best hotel in Marquette, he spotted a familiar face walking into the hotel ... a brutish looking man wearing a black suit and white tie ... with a well-worn fedora slightly tilted on his head. "Where have I seen him before?"

Then he remembered. That's the guy who had been with John Gotti the day Jack witnessed the murder of Louie Castelano. A split second after recognition dawned on him, Jack thought to himself "What's he doing here? This can't be a coincidence!" And he quickly raised the newspaper he had with him to hide from possibly being spotted.

As the bus continued its route, Jack thought about his situation and concluded, "He had to be here looking for me. And if it hadn't been raining so hard," he reasoned, "I would no doubt have been strolling down that stretch of Front Street and would have easily been seen by Gotti's thug. How much does he know? Is he alone?" He trembled at the thought of assassins being so close to their target.

Fortunately, Lakeview was on the outskirts of Marquette, but once home, Jack planned to remain out of sight for a while … just in case. He also decided to contact George early the next morning and see what he knew about 'Mr. Fedora' being in the area.

Later in the day after being contacted by Jack, George was knocking on his door. They sat around the kitchen table and George explained what he knew.

"I'm afraid there's been a breech of our security," he said, "and there are people out there who want to collect on the contract you have on your head. It seems the list of the five locations that were considered for your destination was released to a reporter by mistake. Marquette was on the list and his story about your role in the Gotti trial mentioned those five cities."

"Oh, that's really great," exclaimed Jack. "And were my new name and address mentioned?"

"No, just the five cities," George responded. "They have no way of knowing which city … or where in those cities you might reside. I'm sure all five are being visited to possibly get a line on where you might be. Fortunately, you recognized the thug here in Marquette. That gives you an edge. Just keep your eyes open for his appearance in Lakeview … and stay close to home for a while."

Jack told George, he wasn't comfortable with assassins being so close to his location. He stressed he wanted a more proactive defense of his new life. Jack was concerned that the danger he was in also meant he was putting Alice in danger since they frequently were out and about together.

George said he would figure something out, even if it meant establishing a new life for Jack in another location. Jack stressed any changes would have to consider Alice, since he was not going anywhere without her.

A Plan Comes Together

A few days later, George returned and outlined a plan that would divert the attention of Gotti's assassins to another location. "One of the five cities on the list we released was Tempe, Arizona. We know the thug who is searching that city … Franco Esposito. We want you to travel with us to drop a few tantalizing clues in Tempe that will cause him to report your sighting.

"We want you to help convince Franco that Tempe is where you live in the Witness Protection Program. We want him to spot you several times in the city, and let him follow you to the house in which he will think you reside. We will also let him identify the car you drive and determine your Tempe alias … Jim Parsons."

George continued explaining his plan, "Once he reports back his findings, we expect all those searching the other four cities … including 'Mr. Fedora' … will be drawn to Tempe. You, of course, will be protected at all times, and by the time 'Mr. Fedora' and others arrive you will be long gone.

"This is where it gets tricky," he continued. "We then want Jim Parsons to die. A few days after all the assassins assemble, we'll plant an article in the local newspaper about a car accident and the tragic death of Jim Parsons. We even have an unidentified corpse that's waiting to be found in the burned wreckage of his car … presumably Jim Parsons."

George smiled. "I think we've thought of everything. What do you think?"

"I guess so," Jack said, crossing his fingers.

Truth Comes Out

Back in Lakeview, Jack felt a little more comfortable, but he wanted to celebrate the successful resolution of his 'Mr. Fedora' problem with Alice. He decided to invite her for dinner in his apartment on the evening after his return from Tempe. Jack had been testing several TexMex recipes and was confident that his dinner would be well received … she liked TexMex. He even concocted a respectable frozen

Margarita and a salsa with just the right amount of spiciness. Alice loved it.

They happily sat around after dinner, comfortably holding hands. Jack felt this was the right time to tell Alice about who he really was. The time for secrets had passed. "I've got to tell you about this man you're holding hands with," he said cautiously.

He went on to explain about his marriage, his wife's death, the witnessing of a murder and all the resulting subterfuge leading up to their meeting. He even talked about the close call with 'Mr. Fedora' the previous week. Alice remained quiet during the entire story.

"The federal witness protection program stressed so greatly the importance of my new identity" he said, "that I really came to believe I was Jack Walters, not Jack Evans.

"At the time we met," Jack continued, "I was new to the program and still fearful of Gotti's long arm of retribution. I was a willing subject for doing whatever they said was necessary to stay safe. Last week, I realized how much danger you could be in just by being around me. I'm so sorry I've deceived you. I wouldn't blame you if you just shook your head, threw up your arms, and never spoke to me again."

As Jack said this, he was hoping she had become close enough to him to remain friends ... and maybe become even closer. Jack looked cautiously at her for some reaction … maybe a smile or a twinkle in her eyes. What he got was much more than he could have hoped for.

Alice quietly looked directly into Jack's eyes and lifted her hand to touch his cheek. As she stroked his cheek, she said, "The man I've grown so comfortable with during the past several weeks is not just a name or a history … you are so much more and you have only grown more attractive in my eyes as a result of your admission to what I didn't know about you."

She then took both of Jack's hands in hers and said, "I want to be with you more, not less. I want to help you overcome whatever problems you might have. I want to share what ever time we have left, and to make a home together. Does that sound like I may not want to speak to you again?"

And then she leaned in and gave Jack a gentle kiss. Her smile and twinkling eyes conveyed what Jack was hoping for … and he was thankful they could now share more of themselves as they explored life. He wrapped his arms around her and gave her the biggest hug he could muster … ending with a loving kiss that definitely conveyed his happiness with her desire to make a home together.

Recluse No More

After just three months in Marquette, Jack found he was no longer uncomfortable being Jack Walters. His future looked bright, and his time as the reluctant recluse passed into the past. In his new life, Alice was now a loving partner and together they found that life in Lakeview suited them perfectly.

***

Not to be forgotten, I still have a little ditty ... within 101 words ... featuring our favorite fearsome Brown Recluse Spider........

Feared No More

I'm a spider ... a Brown Recluse to be specific. I'm feared. I live in a closet ... under boxes ... happy. Occasionally, light engulfs my enclosure and a human enters ... withdrawing something hanging above. Such visits are fearsome ... danger seems eminent.

I need a new home. I wander ... searching. Aha, the perfect spot ... a soft, fuzzy slipper ... under the bed ... I enter from above ... comfort and safety together ... ideal!

But then, a human comes close ... my slipper is pulled out ... a human's foot invades my home ... darkness closes in ... my space shrinks ... I'm one with the creature ... feared no more?

***

S is for

Spinster

According to dictionary definitions, spinsters are unmarried women who have aged beyond the usual age for marriage. It draws to mind (in some of us) an image of an older woman, no longer looking for a husband ... often an aunt, teacher or librarian ... with hair severely coiffed in a bun, and with a loveless, prissy or repressed attitude ... often a derogatory image.

In actual fact, spinsters are often more nuanced in their impact on those they encounter. I think of a 7th grade English teacher I had who, I now realize, could have been described as a typical spinster. However, she was sincere, committed, and very good in her efforts to educate (civilize) each of us ... one of my favorite teachers.

It is said that spinsters are often financially well off, or at least happily living within their means. It's the confidence their independent lifestyle (wealth) gives them that enables them to make choices that often seem eccentric to others ... in their friendships, pursuits and attitudes. It's why so many fictional spinsters seem to care so little about the mundane needs of everyday life.

Spinsters have had important roles to play in many novels, movies and television ... even in music. Who can forget Eleanor Rigby ... one of the 'lonely people' who is 'buried along with her name' (never married). Spinsters have a wide range of images in fiction that lend an importance to whatever story is being told ... a role that is often very significant.

On the one hand, there's Miss Marple, Agatha Christie's famous spinster, who uses her charm and understated intelligence to great advantage in solving the most dastardly of crimes. A genial spinster to be reckoned with in numerous novels. A very positive character.

On the other hand, there's Miss Havisham, from Charles Dickens's Great Expectations, an eccentric spinster who has a vengeful heart and a hatred of men. She raises her adopted daughter, Estella, to use her beauty and allure to torment and spurn men in retaliation for being spurned herself at the altar by her fiancé. A not so positive character even though she was overcome with remorse in the final pages.

Something I didn't know ... the term 'thornback' is used by some to designate an unmarried woman in her early 30's and above. To these folks, the term spinster has limited applicability, and as they age they gain the distinguishing title of 'thornback'. Who came up with that, I wonder? Aah … the evolution of language is wonderous!

The term 'spinster' or 'old maid' is also used in the world of sustenance to describe unpopped popcorn kernels. It seems that, like unmarried women who have never had children, the kernels have not 'popped'.

Just how widespread is the idea of unmarried older women as an identifiable class of people? Well, it turns out that women in this group are identified in countries around the world. For example, they are called 'aanissat' in Arabic, 'spinsters' or 'old maids' in English, 'vieilles filles' in French, 'zitelle' in Italian, 'alte Jungfer' in German, 'stara panna' in Polish or 'dakhtar torsheedeh' in Persian. I'd say, spinsters as a group are widely identifiable.

So, now, onward to my story. This chapter is unique (so far) in that there is only one story … and it is a longer tale than usual. It follows 'Sally, the Spinster' on a murder investigation that claimed three lives in the town of Bristol, Tennessee. As was true of Miss Marple, Sally became a key player in bringing the culprit to justice. This is the first 'mystery' in my collection of short stories … and I take a few more pages than usual to tell it.

However, not to be forgotten, I am also adding

another 101-word tale titled 'Silly Spinster Story' ... my attempt in finishing the chapter with a little humor. Oh well, at least I tried.

***

The Spinster and the Bristol Murders

The lane through the wooded park was clouded in darkness as Sally made her way back to her Bristol motel. She was disappointed that the man who she was to meet at the local diner for coffee was a no-show. Although she waited till the last patron had entered, Joel Knight had not arrived.

She was now alone in a strange town in response to a peculiar story from an unknown caller with an unverified accusation. His earnest plea for help, however, eased her normal instincts for caution. As a seasoned reporter for the *Knoxville Times Herald*, she was intrigued.

Sally Simpson had been a reporter at the newspaper for 9 years. She was good at it and had become one of the paper's top reporters. It had consumed her waking hours, and her personal life had suffered as a result. "There's always time for amusements and romance later," she repeatedly told herself.

Now she was in her mid-thirties and unattached ... except to her career. Back at the *Times Herald*, her nickname was 'The Spinster', both because of her apparent lack of interest in marriage and her ability to vividly write her stories as if spinning a tale that really mattered to the reader.

The Game's Afoot

As she walked, she recalled the telephone call, and Joel's story of a potential serial killer in Bristol. He claimed there had been two deaths in his community that had been classified as accidents. "They were murders," he said emphatically, "and there will be at least three more murders in the coming weeks. In fact, I expect the killer will strike again tomorrow and I can tell you who the victim will be."

Sally might have dismissed Joel's call, but she recognized his name as a somewhat well-known author. He had recently published a best-selling novel which, by chance, she had just read.

His call therefore had more credibility and her instincts for a good story caused her to give him leeway to tell her more. He continued, "Tragically, these deaths have not been investigated in spite of my calls urging the local authorities to do so. I need someone who will convince them that my claims could be true, and that they should investigate further."

When Sally asked why he was so certain that these deaths were murders, he replied, "The two people who have already been killed, Frank Devon and Donna Martin, were amateur actors in a local production of an original play called 'The Bristol Murders'. The play ran for two weeks, Friday and Saturday nights, at the Paramount Theater here in Bristol, ending two weeks ago, on June 27th.

"The play is a mystery in which five people die and the local librarian sifts through the clues and identifies the killer in a gathering of suspects in the final scene … sort of like Agatha Christie's Miss Marple might have done.

"The characters played by Devon and Martin were the first two to die in the play and they were killed in the same sequence and in the same manner as in the play … Devon of a drug overdose and Martin from an auto accident. And, in our production, each of the five dead characters was murdered on a Saturday, as were Devon and Martin in real life."

Sally was skeptical, and told Joel, "I'm not convinced you're looking at these deaths objectively, when they could be just a series of coincidences. If the local police aren't finding anything amiss, I would guess there's not much there."

"Well," Joel continued, "there's another, more gruesome possibility that may be more convincing, if it goes that far. If I'm right, Mary Taylor, the third actor who was killed in the play, will die tomorrow … Saturday … of an injury caused in a fall. Surely, there's enough uncertainty here to at least question the authorities on their lack of interest. Someone needs to expose this and end the killer's sinister game."

This conversation had peaked Sally's interest sufficiently that she agreed to meet Joel at the Bristol diner, and she was disappointed when he failed to appear. She was anxious to pursue Joel's theory of foul play in Bristol, Tennessee.

"But why hadn't Joel shown up at the diner?" she asked herself once she was back in her motel room. "He definitely believed that I would be able to help, and would have wanted to see it through."

She was relaxing when her cell phone rang. "Hello," the caller said. "This is Joel Knight and I'm sorry I missed you at the diner, but I'm approaching your room right now and I'd like to have our talk."

The Meeting

As he said this, Sally heard a knock. When she opened the door, she stood face to face with the elusive Joel Knight. "I'm really sorry to have left you waiting at the diner," he said. "I was afraid the killer might be following me and I didn't want to expose you as being associated with my theory on these deaths."

They sat at the table in the corner of her cramped room, and discussed at length Joel's contention that a serial killer was at large. "I am convinced all five actors who died in the play are targets of some mad man. I have no clue as to the motivation of the killer or why the murders are so meticulously planned to seem natural or accidental. And I have no idea who might be perpetrating these killings."

It was then that Joel winced and confided, "But,

since my wife, Linda, is one of the actors targeted in the play … the fifth to die … I implore you to take this seriously and do what ever you can to stop this carefully planned series of murders. I can assure you … personally … those saved will be most appreciative."

As if to emphasize the critical nature of what he was asking, Joel added, "I need someone respected and impartial … you … to convince the authorities to investigate, and to bring their talents and resources to bear on the situation. I don't want any more of our actors to be murdered."

Sally pondered all that Joel was suggesting, and remarked, "Well, it'll be tomorrow morning before we can talk to the people in the Bristol Police Department who need to take action. I know it's late, but let's talk a little bit about who these actors are and what makes them as a group targets … what do they have in common."

Who's Who

"OK," Joel replied. "I'll go down the list and tell you what I know. First of all, our troupe of actors are actors in name only … everyone had a lot of fun pulling together this production, but, no one had any aspirations for pursuing acting any further than the local theater. I think the audience found our play entertaining and got as much a kick out of our energetic but flawed performances as we did." Joel smiled as he recalled their efforts.

"Frank Devon was the first to die. He's in his early 30's," he continued, "and married to Francis, a teller at the Wells Fargo Bank. Acting was a hobby for him … he was actually an agent at State Farm Insurance agency here in town. He was found by his wife on Saturday, July 11th, when she returned home from work. He seemed to be asleep on the couch in the living room, but when Francis tried to wake him, he didn't respond.

"As for the cause of death, the medical authorities found an empty bottle of Percocet nearby and they suspected he took too many … he had broken his arm after the play closed and was prescribed the drug for his pain. They classified his death as resulting from a prescription drug overdose. His character in the play also died of a drug overdose."

Sally asked, "Was their marriage happy … any friction there?"

"They had been married about 10 years and seemingly had a good relationship. Frank was by all appearances devoted to his wife," Joel continued, "and Francis seemed devastated by his death. They don't have any kids … and there was no history of drug dependency and no large insurance pay-out that I'm aware of."

"OK," Sally interjected. "What about Donna Martin?"

"Donna," he replied, "was apparently killed in an auto accident on Saturday, July 18th. Her character in the play also died in an auto accident. She was in her early 20's, and married to Jerry, a doctor in town. Their home was willed to Donna by her parents who died about two years ago."

When Sally asked about how Donna was regarded by others, Joel replied, "She always seemed happy, and she truly enjoyed performing in our play. However, she was a terrible actress, and she would have been the first to tell you she was clumsy on stage. Her outgoing personality and medical knowledge, however, made her the most 'go-to' pharmacist in town."

Joel continued, "Her death was tragic and widely publicized. She apparently was driving too fast along a road just outside of town when her car skidded out of control, plunged down a steep slope and burst into flames. The papers recounted the event, noting that Donna had been cited for two speeding tickets in the last several years."

"Yes," Sally replied, "I remember reading about the accident. So, that brings us to the victim you say will be murdered tomorrow … Mary Taylor. What's her story?"

"Mary is the youngest of the troupe," Joel said. "She is 19, and is what might be called a 'wild child'. She's rough around the edges for someone her age and clearly enjoys life to the fullest. It is said she's a bit of a flirt and 'plays around'... if you know what I mean ... a lot. I know Frank, more than once, complained about her flirtatious behavior.

She wears very 'revealing' clothes ... you know, short skirts ... halter tops ... low cut blouses ... tight tees. As a result, there are always boys traipsing along behind her. She's also an excellent skater, and is seen more often than not roller blading around town wherever she goes."

"Doesn't it seem out of character," Sally asked, "that Mary would find acting in your play appealing? I mean, why did she elect to undertake the many hours required for this play?"

"I think," Joel responded, "she liked the attention lavished on her when she was on the stage. After all, the role she played was simply a caricature of her real life persona. But we all appreciated her affect on ticket sales ... they were up significantly this year, I think, because of her ... 'acting'."

Sally sat back in her chair and thought to herself, "Mary's so different from me. I've always been reserved and introverted in social situations, and committed to whatever goal I am pursuing. I've even heard my cohorts refer to me as 'The Spinster', and I guess it sort of fits."

Sally very much enjoyed her aloofness tendencies and definitely saw herself as a 'Miss Marple' type person. Her career choice to be a reporter was perfect for her in that it allowed her to remain apart from her subjects and be the inquisitor ferreting out the truth. This resulted in a dearth of long-term relationships. "Yep," she thought, "I'm not married ... or even going steady. I really am a spinster."

"The character Mary plays," Joel continued, "was also a skater and she was scripted to be found with her neck broken at the local amusement park. It was suspected she fell climbing up the ferris wheel after the park closed on Saturday ... no doubt to retrieve her skates which were found in one of the higher ferris wheel seats."

"I suggest," Sally said, partly in jest, "that we recommend Mary stay close to home and not go roller blading tomorrow. So, who's next?"

"Grace Watson played the fourth character to die in the play. She is a middle-aged housewife married to Steve, the Wells Fargo VP, who's in his mid 40s. They have one son, about 10 years old. Steve didn't have much to do with the play and came with Grace to rehearsals only rarely.

The character she played was poisoned ... initially it was thought to be a natural death. She was a fairly competent actor and thoroughly enjoyed the theater. Their marriage seemed okay, but they were not what you'd call close ... they largely lived separate lives. If you asked me, I'd say he's going through a mid-life crisis ... although he hasn't purchased a Corvette ... yet."

"Well," Sally said, "I guess that brings us to you, Joel. Tell me a little about Linda's place in this melodrama."

"My wife is a florist," he responded, "and owns her own shop in town. Although she enjoyed her participation in the play, I think she did it more for the opportunity to publicize her business. We've been married for 23 years and look forward to growing old together. No kids.

"In the play," he continued, "Linda dies of food poisoning while eating at her friend's home ... played by Donna. In the real world, they were best friends.

"I'm a writer and work from home. I've published a best-selling novel and several short works, and I'm frequently called upon to write copy for marketing this and that. I help out around the theater whenever asked, creating props needed and helping the director fine tune the script. I've grown to really like the theater and am now thinking I should turn to script writing."

Sally looked up from her notes and asked, "What about any others involved?"

Joel thought a moment, and said, "Well, there's Allen Butler, the director ... this is his first production with the Paramount Theater group. He's come in from New York to direct this production. Apparently he has a lot of experience in the theater, starting out as an actor, but never made it big.

"He's a very intense man and not well liked. In fact, he angrily addressed each actor at various times for their inferior acting skills … he frequently accused them of dragging down the success of 'his' production by not taking advantage of his guidance.

"Then there's Ginger Parker, who plays the librarian … the Miss Marple type of character who solves the murders. She is a first-year actor and probably won't be back in any future plays. Her soft-spoken mannerisms clearly did not reflect the character she was portraying, and the director took particular delight in berating her efforts. She is married, and has no children.

"The only other regular is Paul Minton, the lighting guy, who's sort of a jack-of-all-trades as a result of his early training in the Peace Corps, and he's worked with the Paramount on numerous productions. He's well liked and helps out wherever he's needed. On the side, he's a writer and has entered and won numerous contests for his prose. He also steps in to smaller roles on stage whenever asked."

Sally sat back in her chair and considered other questions to ask. Finally, she said, "I guess that's about all we can do tonight. Let's plan on meeting at the Police Department tomorrow morning at nine. I think we have enough details to convince them to investigate the possibility these two deaths are homicides. Get a good night's sleep … tomorrow is going to be difficult, especially if we can't convince them that there are more deaths coming."

Joel nodded in agreement and turned to leave. "Thank you for taking me seriously. See you tomorrow." The door closed as he departed.

Sally briefly reviewed her notes and frowned as she considered the possibility that a serial killer was loose in the town of Bristol. A few minutes later, she laid down and fell fast asleep.

Detectives At Work

At the Police Department the next morning, they met with Detective Russell Burns and laboriously went over Joel's suspicions and the information they had gathered. He seemed attentive and polite, but skepticism was evident in his expression. Joel didn't make a big deal about having unsuccessfully tried to alert them to this situation earlier in the week, but he did mention it.

When they got to Mary Taylor and their concerns that she was potentially in danger that day, the detective abruptly stopped taking his notes. "Did you say Mary Taylor?" When Joel confirmed her name, he rose from his chair and left the room.

When he returned, he was accompanied by Captain Morse. He looked somberly at Joel, and then at Sally, and said, "Mary Taylor's body was found this morning wearing inline skates at the skateboard park on Elm Street. It was said she was skating after hours on the 'Everton Bowl', a deep bowl named for Josh Everton, a local champion skateboarder, and must have lost her balance. Her neck was broken."

Joel and Sally exchanged glances and Sally said, "That's number three. The killer has struck again. With the predicted death of Mary, you should no longer have any doubts that these are a series of murders, not accidental deaths."

Both detectives now became very pointed in their questions, and urgent in their considerations of actions needed. Sally said very little, letting Joel take the lead, but in her mind she was formulating the article she would have to submit to her paper before the afternoon deadline.

Once they agreed that the three deaths were suspicious and should be examined from that viewpoint, the discussion turned to what motives might be relevant, and who had the opportunity and means to commit the murders.

By the end of the morning, the postmortems on the three victims had been changed to 'likely homicides'. The detectives also acknowledged that the murders were somehow related to the production in which all three victims had played roles.

Over the next several days, they began interviewing those associated with the play. Based on the insights gleaned from those discussions, they widened their interviews to spouses and close friends.

Sally had become a frequent participant in their investigations by agreeing to not publish anything else on the case beyond the initial article she filed after her first talk with Joel. They didn't want her printed speculations on 'who-done-it' to muddy the waters as they zeroed in on the killer. After an arrest, she would then have the exclusive rights to tell the story.

In actual fact, they were happy to have Sally's instincts at work as they sorted through the evidence which would help solve the case. They were a small police department with limited resources. Her importance to discern the truth and to know when what's not said is important, honed over the years as a reporter, helped the detectives immeasurably. As a result of her participation, they were able to develop further avenues for investigation which eventually led to finding the killer.

Findings

As a result of their interviews and further investigations, the following observations were made. While not all had a direct bearing on solving the murders, they each reflected motives that had to be pursued.

1. The group boasted not one, but two sets of extramarital affairs … a regular 'Peyton Place'. Jerry Martin had regularly met Ginger Parker every Friday

at the same motel where Sally was staying, while their spouses were occupied at the Paramount. They were very serious and had toyed with ideas on how to make their relationship permanent. It was theorized that Jerry could have killed their spouses to further that goal, and then set up other murders to distract attention from their involvement.

2. The second set of adulterers involved Steve Watson and Francis Devon. They had several sexual get-togethers during the length of the production, and enjoyed their interludes together. While it didn't seem like they had long-term intentions, as did Jerry and Ginger, they were very passionate and one or the other could have perpetrated the killings.

3. Donna Martin's driving recklessness had angered at least one of the group. She had nearly run Steve Watson off the road on one occasion after following him closely for several miles, honking for him to let her pass. Steve was furious over this incident and complained bitterly to anyone who would listen. This could have led him to include Donna as a murder target, along with the husband of his paramour, Francis. There may have been others who harbored similar resentments that might have led to her demise.

4. Allen Butler, the director, was not an easy man to get along with. But he was also affected by what he considered inferior actors in 'his' play and he regularly berated their efforts. Some would describe

him as passionately resentful of their shortcomings and say that he took it very personally. He was definitely borderline psychotic in his belief that they made 'his' production less than perfect. It's a small jump from being passionate to being murderously protective. But then, again, he might also have been the target of murder by any of the actors he berated.

5. Mary Taylor created much tension ... and passion ... in the people around her. Some resented her flirting with their spouses, and others were offended that she spurned their advances. She was a spark plug for inciting passionate feelings that may have led to her being murdered. Jerry was threatened by the possibility she would reveal his relationship with Ginger ... and his spurned advances to her. Joel had also flirted with Mary and he resented her laughter when he suggested a romantic dalliance. There might also have been several bitter wives who resented her flirting.

6. Joel Knight was a successful writer, and, like many successful people, he was somewhat of an egotist. His wife, Linda, cringed every time Joel began boasting about his best selling novel, and was personally humiliated by his frequent disparaging remarks about her 'uninspired' floral arrangements. Was she motivated to kill her husband? She didn't seem the type, but who knows?

7. Frank Devon was a wife abuser. His wife, Francis, had needed medical attention several times as a result

of 'falls' in her home. Many of her friends knew of her situation, and warned her that she shouldn't put up with it. However, Frank was always apologetic and sought forgiveness, and she wanted to believe he still loved her, so no help was sought. Even her doctor, Jerry, urged her to seek help, and offered to intercede on her behalf. Certainly, both Francis and Jerry had sufficient reason to rid the world of another wife abuser.

In addition to these reasoned observations, the crime scene investigators and medical examiners provided the following forensic evidence from the scene of each murder. While it had been reported that these deaths were now considered homicides, none of the specifics uncovered by the forensics team had been released.

1. Frank Devon had died two weeks before his death was considered a homicide, but they were able to collect three clues linked to his murder. First, there were two wine glasses at the scene that had traces of a red wine. Fingerprints on one were Frank's, but the other glass had Jerry Martin's prints. Second, cyanide was found in Frank's system and was ruled as the cause of death, but there were no traces of this poison in Frank's wine glass. Third, Frank's body was posed to reflect the exact position of his death scene in the play.

2. Donna Martin had died a fiery death in the driver's seat of her car. The examination of the car

revealed that the brake line had been severed and was no doubt the cause of the accident. There were no fingerprints, but it was determined that she was driving away from the Paramount Theater on her fateful trip. Her telephone was found and it revealed that she had received a call before her departure from a room at a resort just out of town. The room had been rented by Allen Butler ... and the caller suggested Donna meet him at the resort ... and the resort was in the direction in which she was heading when the accident occurred.

3. Mary Taylor's neck was broken, but on closer examination, faint bruising around her neck was inconsistent with the break having been caused by a fall. She had all the markings of her having been strangled from behind with a length of rope. It was also revealed that Mary only skated on relatively level surfaces and never visited the skateboard park ... the 'Everton Bowl' would have terrified her.

Inductive Reasoning

As Sally, Detective Burns, and Captain Morse considered all these elements of the crimes, they began to hypothesize as to who might have committed the murders.

"Well, let's start by eliminating anyone who could not be involved based on what we know" said Sally. "Obviously, the three victims can be eliminated. Likewise, Grace Watson, Linda Knight and Ginger

Parker are unlikely since they were next in line to die if the suspected trend held true. That leaves five possibilities: Francis Devon, Jerry Martin, Steve Watson, Joel Knight, and Allen Butler. What do you think?"

Detective Burns shook his head and noted, "I can't see Francis Devon as the killer. While she could have handled the poisoning of her husband, I wouldn't think she could strangle Mary or be able to sever the brake line of Donna's car. Wasn't she described as being a rather weak personality with soft-spoken mannerisms? I'd say she's a very long shot."

Captain Morse interjected, "You'd be surprised at what the quiet types are capable of … especially when they've been abused! But I can't say I'd disagree in this case. So now we're down to four suspects."

"I'd also rule out Jerry Martin," Sally said, "Not because he couldn't do it, but because as a doctor he's committed to saving lives. While he might want to rid the world of Frank because of his abuse of Francis, I don't see him as being able to murder the others just to cover his tracks."

The two detectives agreed. "Well, that leaves three," said Sally. "And I would also eliminate Joel Knight from consideration simply because he fought so hard to get this investigation started. These deaths were considered accidents before he raised a ruckus and we all took another look. Also, his resentment of Mary's laughter at him for his advances is a rather weak motive for multiple killings."

"So, we're down to two suspects now," noted Detective Burns.

"I suggest that Allen Butler also be dropped from our list," suggested Captain Morse. "While he was certainly passionate about 'his' play, it would seem more likely that he would have been the target for death by almost anyone in the production, rather than being the perpetrator of the killings. His demand for doing things 'his' way is well documented in his history of directing other plays, and they did not evolve into murder."

"That would sort of narrow down our list of potential killers to just Steve Watson," observed Detective Burns. "Is he our killer?"

"I'm dubious," Sally replied. "His short-term fling with Francis Devon would not seem to validate the extreme act of multiple killings. Especially when he has a young son at home and a responsible position at the Wells Fargo Bank."

"Well, we're down to no obvious suspects now," noted Burns. "This is tough! Any further thoughts?"

"I'd like to go back to the director," said Sally. "True, he was not a favorite among the production team, and could easily have been the victim of their resentment, but he's the only one who verbally … and passionately … abused everyone who was in the cast. He might blame them all for the play not being a greater success. Wasn't he described as being 'borderline psychotic' and 'resentful of their shortcomings' … that he took their failures 'very personally'? He's my number one suspect!"

"OK," said Captain Morse. "Assuming he's guilty, how do we proceed from here? How do we prove or disprove he committed the murders?"

The Proof of the Pudding Is in the Eating

"I've got an idea," said Sally, and the detectives perked up. "I'd like to interview Allen, the self-described prominent director, for my newspaper and provoke him to say something incriminating. I think he's such an egotist that he won't be able to resist the chance to be in the spotlight, and, with the right prodding, might just let slip details only the killer would know."

Both detectives nodded, and Burns said, "I have nothing better to suggest that wouldn't cause him to 'lawyer-up' and be on guard. We need to do something if he's our guy, because he'll be returning to New York at the end of the week."

Captain Morse agreed and said, "That might just work. I'll coordinate with Larry Moss, the prosecuting attorney. He'll want to be involved to make sure we don't step on some legal technicality. How would you like to set this up?"

They decided that Sally would arrange to meet Allen

for a private interview at the Paramount the next afternoon. She called him and he jumped at the chance to discuss his career and his latest play for the *Knoxville Times Herald*. He no doubt was thinking it might also be syndicated to larger markets around the country. He took the bait.

What Allen didn't know was that the location of the interview was selected and specifically configured so that the interview could be secretly video taped. The two detectives and the prosecuting attorney would be in a back room, out of sight, where they would be able to watch the entire session.

All of the setup was overseen by Larry, since he would be the attorney handling any resulting prosecution. He cautioned them, "We need to avoid the appearance of entrapment … let him ramble on as much as possible.

"Sally," he cautioned, "your questions must not appear to be leading him to say something incriminating. What he volunteers is what's going to be acceptable to the courts. Just proceed with the interview as you would any other celebrity."

The Interview

When Allen showed up at the theater for the interview, Sally was there and welcomed him with a big smile. "Come on in, Allen. To make you more comfortable, I'd like to conduct the interview on stage where you directed your most recent success.

"By the way," Sally continued, "I usually record my interviews, if it's ok with you." He nodded in agreement. "I will also be taking extensive notes. I may ask you to slow down now and then so I'm sure to get relevant factors correct in my notes."

Allen grinned in appreciation of her consideration, and they moved to where a table and chairs had been set up for their use. Once comfortable, Sally began her interview with questions about his early years in the theater and Allen responded at length with glowing accounts of his acting experiences.

Sally oohed and aahed as he recounted in self-congratulatory terms his work on the stage, eventually leading him to discuss his efforts in producing and directing various projects. She stopped him occasionally and asked him to expand on what he was telling her. He sensed that her attention was riveted on what he was saying.

"So," Sally continued, "I understand your most recent project, an original play called 'The Bristol Murders', was a resounding success here at the Paramount. Ticket sales greatly exceeded any previous production … no doubt due to your very professional directing."

"Well," he responded, "the local critics said it was a success. But, I was actually very disappointed in the production. It was not an easy project. It never is when you're working with a group of amateurs. And these amateurs fell well short of being acceptable.

I'm afraid I had to be their Dutch uncle … pushing them all along the way. You know, you can't be best friends to a cast when your reputation for excellence is on the line."

After talking for a while about his commitment to bringing out the best in his cast, Sally turned the conversation to the individual actors. "Allen, let's talk a little bit about the tragic deaths of three actors in your production. It looks like the police have determined that they were murders, not accidents. Why do you suppose the killer focused on your play for his grisly crimes?"

Allen looked calmly at Sally and replied, "Who knows? Probably just to attract more attention to his deed. He must be crazy. But, it's hard to sympathize with the victims … all three were thorns in my side and never appreciated the direction I was giving them throughout the play's run."

Sally looked puzzled and asked, "You can't mean that they deserved to die as a result of their acting in your play?"

"No," he responded, "but I can understand the frustration they inflict on others. Take Frank, for example. He spent more time fretting about his insurance business than he did on refining his character in the play. I'm sure the killer was a disgruntled claimant who was just as angry about his lack of focus as I was.

"It would certainly have been easy," he continued, "for anyone to slip a little cyanide into something Frank ate. I'm sure his passing must have made someone very happy," he said smiling. "And being that he was posed in death just as he had been in the play simply means the killer had a sense of humor and had seen the play."

Sally sat across the table from Allen and focused intently as he responded to her questions. He sensed that she was listening in admiration of his every word. Her sense was that the story was coming together and it made her grin. "This story is going to make 'The Spinster' a household name," she thought to herself.

Allen continued with even more fervor, "And, as to Donna, her road rage and pushy ways irritated many in town who would think her death in an auto accident was justly deserved. A little snip of the brake line was all it would take. And by luring her to an out of town destination, she would have been on a stretch of road where brake failure would have been catastrophic."

Then Sally turned to the third victim, "Surely, Mary's death was not deserved. She was so young."

"Well," he responded. "She was a total disruption to my play ... flirting like she did with every man who came near. And what a fitting end ... to die showing off her skating skill in that park she and her buddies played in."

He continued with an angry aside. "I wouldn't be surprised, however, if she was actually killed by a spurned suitor who snuck up behind her with a length of rope and strangled her and left her to die alone. A suitable end!"

Allen angrily offered one final commentary on the murders: "I wouldn't be at all surprised if there are more deaths of cast members over the next several weeks. The killer seems to be on a roll. And they all deserved what they got for not taking more seriously their participation in my play."

The Arrest

Sally sat back in her chair and relaxed. "Well, Allen … I guess that does it. I think I have enough for my story now. Thank you very much!"

Allen smiled with pride as he envisioned a glowing article on his career … a major force in the theater. He would get the recognition he so richly deserved.

Just then, he heard the a door open and footsteps approaching their table. He turned around, and stood to greet the three men who had listened to his entire interview … an interview that confirmed his guilt as the murderer.

Detective Burns roughly turned Allen around and pulled his arms behind him … slipping handcuffs on his wrists. "Allen Butler … you're under arrest for murder of Frank Devon, Donna Martin, and Mary

Taylor. You have the right to remain silent. Anything you say can and will be used against you in a court of law."

Burns could be heard continuing to 'Mirandize' Allen as he was escorted out of the theater, "You have the right to an attorney. If you cannot afford an attorney, one will be provided for you. Do you understand the rights I have just read to you?"

Sally slowly stood and watched as Allen was led away. Captain Morse stayed behind and quietly said, "Sally … you did good! We certainly have enough from your interview to hold him and I'm sure we'll find corroborating evidence as we dig further into these murders."

Then he said, "You can take a great deal of pride in stopping what could have been even more deaths. He was just getting started. Thanks to you and Joel, we had reason to investigate these deaths as homicides before any other victims piled up. And your interview of Allen was brilliant and gave us the ammunition we needed to prosecute the case."

She smiled at the compliment, and immediately thought of Joel. As Captain Morse left, she placed a call to Joel and asked if he would meet her at the diner. "We never did have a cup of coffee there, and I understand they make the best apple pie in the Southeast."

He agreed to meet and, once together, she again

thanked him for insisting that these deaths be investigated. "You're the true hero in this case ... you saved several lives and helped bring the killer of the Bristol Murders to justice. You need to know that your role will be emphasized in any account of this case I write."

Then Sally said her goodbyes, got in her car and headed south to Knoxville ... to home.

The Headline

Sally was able to publish her articles on the Bristol Murders, and her stories were widely circulated. Her coverage was even nominated for a Pulitzer Prize for Investigative Reporting that year.

While her reporting on Allen Butler's crimes provided a factual account of the investigations and the solving of the murders, her headline for the final article was what her readers found particularly appropriate ...

The Butler Did It!

... The 'Spinster' had always wanted to say that!

***

Not to be forgotten, here's a silly ditty ...
within 101 words ... about Susan the Spinster.

Silly Spinster Story

Susan says strange stuff. She's startled seeing several surreal scarabs symbolizing sacred sacraments. Such sacrilege saddens Susan severely since spinsters supposedly stay staid ... succinct salient scenarios suspiciously seduce serious scholars since such stories seem sleazy.

Whew......

Susan studies social solutions sounding somewhat sophisticated ... struggling souls seem superficially situated singularities. Scholars see such sordid symbols signifying serious situations silently ... singers sing songs shunning such sleazy stuff.

Subsequently, sleepy Susan says sensitive spinsters sense such situations somewhat suspiciously since sleep sustains such sweet sorrows. Soothingly, several studies say sleaze should stay silent, sending spinster's sensibilities soaring.

Sensible ?

Silly !!!

T is for Trump

While considering what word to select for this chapter, I thought about 'tractor', 'trumpet', 'tedious', and 'torment'. However, how could I not choose 'trump' after living through the four years of the Donald Trump era. There has never been a more tumultuous period in my memory, and surely I have much to say in that regard. Of course, 'trump' was selected ... and now I just have to create a story line or three for the 'T is for Trump' chapter.

The dictionary defines 'trump' in terms related to card games ... "a playing card of the suit chosen to rank above the others, which can win a trick where a card of a different suit has been led". But it can also be used in terms of gaining dominance in other situations ... "a valuable resource that may be used, especially as a surprise, in order to gain an advantage".

So, my stories are not limited to those involving

Donald Trump or his presidency. But, hey … would anyone expect I would write about anything else?

In actual fact, I spent several days doing just that. I had drafted a twelve page tale titled, 'A Man Named Trump' in which I exposed my opinions to create a tale of intrigue. It began …

> *"This is a story of politics and intrigue … success and failure. It explores what impact a political outsider can have on a country's orbit in national and international affairs … an exciting tale in which all involved have an opinion or two. In fact, the divisiveness engendered is at the heart of my story."*

It goes on from there to explore and opine about the impact 'the Donald' had on our country and every person in it. However, on rereading the draft … several times … I felt it was too literal and personal … too political … and should not be a part of my collection of short stories.

So, now what could I do with my chapter once I had decided to avoid the most consequential subject revolving around the word: 'trump'.

When all else fails, my recourse to writing is to … just start with whatever thoughts first come to mind. In this case, my first thoughts revolved around a grim reaper named Harold, and a bridge game played by long deceased ancestors of mine.

Of course, you may infer from my first thoughts

whatever you might ... but I might consider them a little weird.

Now, to make things a little more weird, your old codger has changed his mind on the tale at first rejected. I decided as I finished the layout of this chapter that perhaps 'the Don' shouldn't be avoided in a chapter tailor-made for him. So, 'A Man Named Trump' is back in ... somewhat edited and abbreviated ... but you can judge whether it's worth while or not.

***

The Trump Card

My name is George and I'm an 81 year old 'survivor' of aging. At this age, I have the best possible perspective on life's perilous journey. I'd like to share what I've experienced in my life to give you a little better idea of the challenges all living creatures endure ... some for shorter durations than others, and some with greater suffering than others.

No one said life is supposed to be easy, but we learn that truth over time. It comes with ferocity for many and quiet certitude for the rest of us. For me, at 81, it's been a gradual understanding that the grim reaper ... I call him Harold ... waits just around the bend in life, weighing the worth of my existence. It amuses him while he considers whether or not to trump my life and curtail any future I might have.

I use the term 'trump' when it comes to shortening a persons longevity as a euphemism for death ... the final act of life ... the weapon eventually used by the grim reaper on all of us. As in many card games, the trump card is able to stop progress toward an objective. In life, when Harold plays his trump card, someone dies.

There have been many times in my life when I felt Harold's presence, and was relieved that he held back that trump card. I often wondered what he saw when he elected to restrain the temptation to cause my death. Did he see some glorious future ahead for me, some personal worth in letting me live, or was he just curious about what was down the road I trod?

But enough of the overview of what this tale is about. Basically, it comes down to being a story of my recollections when I sensed my age was getting the better of me … when Harold's trump card was withheld and I lost a bit more of my 'old' self.

I guess my first encounter with the reality of my body's frailty was when as a pre-teen I was rushed to the hospital for a tonsillectomy. The bad sore throat that prompted my move to surgery, however, was not what caused me to think I was dying. Rather it was the much more severe pain afterward when, looking back, I sensed Harold's first appearance and, as a kid, I thought I might succumb. Well, obviously, the trump card was not played and I credit the soothing effects of icy cold strawberry ice cream for thwarting Harold's hand.

Now, you might think that having tonsils removed is routine with little lasting damage to the body, but as a 12 year old having never been seriously sick … sick enough to be rushed to the hospital … it was terrifying and caused trauma far beyond simply the removal of what this body had been born with. It left the question in my mind … "Am I to be subjected to other health maladies in my future … will I survive?"

Thereafter, as an active teenager, I lived as though the early warning of my fragility was simply a quirk and that I was immune from the effects of wear and tear on my body. I ran everywhere, took stairs two or three steps at a time, climbed trees, jumped around, played a ton of basketball and other sports ... I never sensed that the frequent blisters and leg cramps were Harold's warning that I should be more careful.

Sometimes the assault on maintaining a harm-free life resulted from total recklessness. Such was the case when I suffered a broken knuckle during a schoolyard skirmish with a buddy of mine. It taught me that slight mishaps can have a lasting affect on daily living ... and perhaps on long-term confidence in my ability to protect this body from harm as well.

The cast I wore on my right hand (I'm right handed) ... from fingertips to elbow ... for three weeks ... caused consternation and embarrassment as I grappled with schoolwork and testing in the final days of the 7th grade. Now, my handwriting has ever been a strong point of my dubious talents, but it's a wonder the teachers could decipher my scribbles as I switched to writing with my left hand. I'm sure even Harold got a kick out of watching my valiant efforts.

And did I mention the 'itch'? Invariably my hand encased in the cast developed a persistent itch that caused much discomfort ... and prompted me to find ingenious ways to scratch it ... not at all easy considering the area was covered with a plaster cast. I used a back scratcher that was fairly efficient ... and a wire coat hanger bent to slip under the cast ... but none of the devices used provided total relief. At least it was a distraction from my struggles with being a southpaw.

Sometimes the onslaught to my body resulted from pure stupidity. One of my assignments in the Army was to a remote post located in Sinop, Turkey, on the coast of the Black Sea. When I say 'remote', I mean really isolated, with very little to occupy the off-duty time of a young adult in his prime. One thing they did have, however, was an NCO Club that offered 10 cent drinks. Harold perked up and smiled broadly at what this could result in.

Now, I was never a drinker. Even at college fraternity parties, I chose soda over beer … and nothing in lieu of the hard stuff. But, at 10 cents a drink, and nothing much else to do, camaraderie demanded evenings of festive hoisting one or two … or more … sometimes too many more. I distinctly remember three Saturdays when I learned a thing or two about alcohol.

One memory was of a day when a group of us enjoyed a Saturday afternoon playing basketball on our outside makeshift dirt court. The day was beautiful and our unit seemed to play inspired ball … and we upset the favored team. In the excitement of winning, we gathered at the club to cool off and celebrate. Someone ordered a round of beers … and then another. It was ice cold and tasted great. By the time I stopped to think about what after effects might be in the offing, I found myself ordering another round … and then another … and then, I have difficulty remembering the end of the evening. But, the next morning I awoke on my bunk, still in my fatigues, with my head throbbing. One thing was clear, however, I felt compelled to attend church service … for the first time since my arrival.

The second learning experience followed several weeks later, after an afternoon of swimming and relaxing at the local beach. Again, it was a beautiful day … the water was cool, the sand warm, and our group had the shore to ourselves. A local 'merchant' came by peddling various local delicacies from his horse-drawn cart. One of the guys jumped up, saying, "Have you ever tasted any of the local red wine … it's really pretty good." Well, he bought several jugs and, being curious and thirsty, we all gave it a try. Not bad, but I was hardly a connoisseur. What I do know, however, is that by later that evening … after continued sipping on that intoxicating red wine … memory again began to fade and I awoke the next morning wanting two or three aspirin … and the calming ambience of church once more.

The third memory I have of drinking in Turkey occurred after a 24 hour shift when our unit decided to grab a bite to eat and relax at the NCO Club. It was late Saturday afternoon and we were all exhausted. We should have retired and readied ourselves for the next afternoon's assignment, but …

NOOOO!!!!… we just had to let our hair down a bit. The club was out of beer that evening, but they had a special going on mixed drinks. Now, 10 cents is a great price, but when they drop the price to a nickel, who can resist? I ordered a screwdriver thinking, 'It's an orange juice drink … it can't be too bad!" But, after my fifth, I changed my opinion and declared, "These drinks will be my ruination … I'll have another, bartender!" The next morning … severe headache … memory lapses … off to church, again.

Now, I feel like I've learned a lesson or two from these three experiences. I learned that beer, red wine, and screwdrivers can be quite refreshing in moderation, and quite painful if enjoyed in excess. Harold must've laughed and laughed as I experienced their aftereffects. However, for a young man, this was an important lesson. I'm not so sure he appreciated my response the morning after … but the main appreciation I gained was that: I did survive … both the drinking and the isolation in Turkey.

One of my other encounters with Harold came during happier moments in my life. For example, while romancing my future bride in my late 20s, I experienced sharp pains in my lower abdomen (not a cause and effect situation) … I just knew this was a precursor to a stroke or heart attack or one of those other serious maladies that old people talk about. As I was being checked in to the hospital for an emergency appendectomy, the pain only intensified. I could sense Harold grinning at my bedside. Would this be when his trump card would descend on my future as I slowly lapsed into unconsciousness?

Well, I awoke gradually in the recovery room with my mom, sister, and bride-to-be hovering around me. As it turned out, Harold had withdrawn the trump card for later use as he watched the attentiveness of those at my side. I've been told that during the peak of my semiconsciousness, my attention was riveted on my fiancée-to-be as I groggily expressed undying love for her.

I credit those moments of honest expressions for strengthening my efforts to bring us together … my quest for gaining her 'yes' to my marriage proposal was accomplished shortly thereafter. Could it be that Harold was persuaded that playing the trump card was premature when he heard those genuine words of love? That's my bet! However, it was another reminder that my body was fragile and subject to wearing out.

Sometimes, the impact of aging was experienced in a less dramatic fashion, although with a much more serious potentiality … and a grinning Harold simply watched from a distance. That was the case when I woke one day in my mid-30s in fright … my left eye was impaired and a growing black spot was partially blocking my vision. Not wanting to panic my bride (yes, Virginia, my fiancée is now my wife), I simply mentioned that I had a problem. She simply responded to my depiction of worsening vision with an emphatic, no-nonsense order … "We're going to the eye doctor … NOW!"

Well, we were at the ophthalmologist an hour later … the spot was getting larger … and the doctor said, "We're going to surgery, NOW! You have a detached retina and it'll get much worse if we wait. Blindness in that eye is a distinct possibility." An hour later, I was undergoing an emergency laser repair of that eye … and the right eye was also preemptively treated while he was at it. While Harold was not present at my side for this assault on my presumed invincibility, it was another close call that reminded me that I was not so invincible after all.

At this point in my life, it was beginning to sink in that bad things do happen to good people - I considered myself in that category - and I'd better be more careful. It was also a time when I began recognizing how each passing day was a gift not to be taken for granted … life was indeed good and very much worth enjoying.

However, I knew Harold and his trump card would continue to be a threat. But I sensed that if there were a grim reaper, there also had to be a Creator involved. With the frailty of my life now a certainty, the importance of soliciting help from the Creator seemed prudent. My belief in God began to play an even more important role as I continued to meander down life's highway.

Harold returned with a vengeance in my mid-40s when I began suffering from severe pains in my lower back. The pain gradually increased over time. Some days the pain struck with a sudden jolt and a ferocity that caused me to stop whatever I was doing … it was difficult to stand or sit … some days I simply had to stay in bed. I could envision Harold preparing to play his trump card.

Doctors were consulted and they tried to help, but nothing seemed to work. I was hospitalized several times as they applied traction, but any favorable results didn't last long. Physical therapy was of little use. Injections of this and that didn't help. Pain relievers and muscle relaxants, both over-the-counter and prescription strengths, were less effective than I would have liked. While there were temporary periods when the pain seemed to be under control, it always eventually reappeared … sometimes at the most inopportune times.

Then in 1988, doctors recommended surgery. This came as a result of a painful trip by car my bride and I took from our home in Virginia to Dallas, Texas, for a convention. While there, I experienced a sudden series of back spasms that were truly debilitating. On the first day, we walked as far as the hotel lobby and a jolt of pain stopped me … I literally couldn't move … couldn't sit … couldn't stand. My bride leaned me against a column and went for help. She came back with a wheelchair and I was wheeled to our room.

Well, the conference became moot at this point and,

after a painful night, we checked out at 4:00 a.m. or so and began our 'hellish drive' home. I couldn't help with the driving and laid reclined in the passenger seat for the entire trip ... moaning as we travelled down roads with an amazing number of potholes and bumps. We stopped at a motel after an all day drive to give my bride a rest. But my pain was such that we decided to get back on the road after an hour or two. My wife was an angel for taking care of me on this trip ... I was not an ideal patient.

Surgery had never been recommended because x-rays and MRI scans couldn't locate a problem that was treatable with surgery. The severity of pain from our trip to Dallas and the increasing frequency of bouts, however, convinced them they should go in and take a look. So once again, Harold was at my side as I slid into unconsciousness, and doctors did their exploratory surgery.

I awoke sometime later in the recovery area and, for the first time in many months, realized there was no pain. Harold was nowhere to be seen. The doctors explained that they had found a broken disk in my spine, and that one piece had lodged against a nerve. They removed it and worked more of their magic which they predicted would itself eliminate the back pain. And that's generally been the case ever since. However you can bet, I've been very cautious since then in limiting the stress on my back.

On rereading what I've written thus far, you might

get the impression that I've lived a life in terrible agony caused by ailments of various kinds. Well, like many others, I have had to deal with health issues, but I am most fortunate in that none have been totally debilitating and that there have been welcome remedies. Overall, I have only encountered Harold infrequently and have been able to push him to the side and live an enviable life.

However, in 2009, in my late-60s, a really scary encounter occurred. A bad number popped up on one of the tests run during my annual physical that hinted of prostate cancer. I was off to a specialist and various tests, including a biopsy of my prostate gland which confirmed the cancer and led to marking the gland for radiation treatments ... none of which were pleasant. And then there were the radiation sessions that followed ... 8 weeks of daily treatments ... non-painful but very boring.

The treatments were scheduled to begin at 8:00 a.m. each morning ... Monday through Friday. Upon arrival, I was positioned on a 'slab' in this gigantic 'machine'. My position was precisely situated so that the radiation rays struck their target. Then the machine was switched on and began bumping and grinding in an orbit around my body as the radiation worked its magic from various directions. It was an eerie experience.

But it worked, and Harold was thwarted again. I've been clear of any recurrence for over ten years now

… fingers crossed.

I guess I should mention the various afflictions that gained prominence as my advancing age took their toll. What can I say … well, certainly, aches and pains have gradually intensified as I added years to my age. And the extra pounds that I have added make me question whether satisfying my taste buds was worth it.

My knees, in particular, began 'screaming' louder as routine walking, standing, and just getting up and down, became more and more painful. Pain relievers like Tylenol became ineffective and only Advil seemed to work, somewhat … and my doctor warned that I shouldn't take Advil with the other meds I was taking. What to do … what to do? No choice … use the pain reliever that works … in moderation.

In addition, my hearing became more questionable with clarity of what was being said becoming a problem. I was certainly saying, "What?" more and more often. Even calluses on my feet appeared and painfully reminded me with each step that this body doesn't have too many more miles on it. I also now walk with a cane to assist with occasional dizziness and balance issues that have become more prevalent. And did I mention I had to have surgery to remove cataracts on both eyes?

Perhaps, I surmise, I didn't care for this body as well as I should have.

I guess there are very few parts of this old body that haven't shown signs of wearing out. Oh, well … on the plus side, I haven't seen Harold around for a while. And my bride and I continue to lead happy and fruitful lives, thanks largely to having family close by to help and encourage us.

Looking back, life has been good! But, at this age, I wonder if Harold and his trump card are too far away.

However, don't mourn for me. I've been given every consideration in this life. Harold more than once has withheld the final playing of the trump card … giving me a future in my youth and adult life that I wouldn't trade for anything. I'm sure there will be more serious encounters with Harold in the years ahead. After all, at 81 you might say I'm now living on borrowed time.

But, do I really think there's a Harold at my side who takes a special interest in my well-being? Or is it simply a matter of fate? Probably just fate … however, I sort of like the idea of having Harold there to debate the merits of my passing. I do feel blessed that I've survived this long … my various medical encounters aside.

It's going to be interesting to see whether I go out after a prolonged illness … can't be too drawn out at my age … or quickly in my sleep. I certainly vote for the latter!

***

A Ghostly Bridge Game

S it back and I'll tell you a tale about four ethereal ladies ... from a world that once was ... who met periodically to play a ghostly game of bridge. I don't know from whence they came ... they were from different times and places ... and their memories and perspectives were quite their own. The one thing they had in common was that they each married a Gildersleeve, and were thus distant relatives of mine.

For whatever reason, I understood they met thusly over time to share favorite stories and to commiserate on their fates ... and, of course, to play bridge. I know it may be difficult to believe, but I can attest to the one gathering I witnessed ... but it's beyond me to explain how it happened.

As to the four ladies at the center of my tale. I should mention that everything I'm about to tell you about them is as it appeared to me ... I do not vouch for its veracity ... or even the reality of what I believe I saw. I found it all most mysterious, as I'm sure you will, but it is as it was in my viewing ... be it an apparition, hallucination, or simply me degenerating into madness.

Of course, my ladies are from a time of which I have no knowledge, so listen with skepticism. I say this because their names are actually the real names of ancestors in my family tree so you might infer all is as it was. Here's what I observed … or sensed. Take it for what it's worth.

The first bridge player was Dorcas Williams. She lived in the mid-to-late-17th Century and married my great, great, great, great, great, great, great grandfather, Richard Gildersleeve, Jr., in 1654. Dorcas seemed above average in intellect, with a bit of pretentiousness that comes with a higher station in life. Her clothes were well tailored and reflected the high styles of London from where she immigrated as a young adult.

Her partner at the bridge table was Experience Ellison who married Richard Gildersleeve, 3rd, the son of Dorcas and Richard. They lived in the late-17th early-18th Centuries. She had a calm demeanor and reflected the street smarts of someone who grew up and had to cope with the challenges of frontier life. Her appearance was rough-hewn, both in her apparel and physical features.

The third player was Mary Dinge, who lived in the late-18th Century. She married Obadiah Gildersleeve, the grandson of Richard and Experience. She was smart and practical, and was of great assistance to her husband in his business and political ventures. She exhibited a sense of pride in their accomplishments and an eagerness to tackle whatever life threw at her … she was fearless.

Temperence Gibbs was the fourth player … bridge partner to Mary. She married Philip Gildersleeve, the son of Mary and Obadiah, and they lived in the late-18th early-19th Centuries. Contrary to her name, Temperence did not shy away from an occasional alcoholic drink and she was a frequent companion with her husband at local taverns. While her temperament was frequently impulsive and imprudent, her natural instincts were more often unerring. Her dress was casual and what might be considered common to social norms. She smiled a lot.

So there we have it. Four ladies from different times, gathered around a table set up in the center of a room for a game of bridge. The time was uncertain … the place was undistinguished in any manner … and there were no others in the area. The room itself had walls that seemed hazy, but were opaque to the eye, and there were no other furnishings. Looking up, I could see there was no ceiling … just far-off wisps of clouds floating in a starlit night. The ladies all appeared anxious to get play underway.

Bridge is appropriate as a setting for their get-togethers. It has long been both a game of skill, and a common excuse for social interaction. It evolved from the British game of whist, which was first played in the 16th Century. My four ancestors picked up the fundamentals of bridge easily from their skill in playing whist, and it became their game of choice sometime before the gathering I witnessed.

"Let's get this game underway," exclaimed Mary.

"Our time grows short and I'm anxious to see how this day's play ends up. Temperence and I won on our last visit and I have a feeling we're going to continue that trend. Dorcas, you dealt, so lead away!"

"Hold on there, Mary," responded Experience. "One day's play doesn't make for a trend. I've a feeling today will be disappointing for you and Temperence. By the way, Mary, you never did tell us why you and Obadiah had to move suddenly to Sag Harbor in 1762 ... a little trouble with the authorities?"

"You know very well we moved to take advantage of a ship-building opportunity," responded Mary ... "which, by the way, fared much better than Richard's efforts in the militia."

Dorcas interrupted and said, "Mary ... Experience ... stop this wrangling and let's get on with our game. As dealer, I bid 1 heart." It seems they were all aware of each other's strengths and weaknesses, and which buttons to push to cause a response. As I watched, the smiles and laughter around the table grew more lusty as barbs were traded and the friendships formed over time were renewed.

The bidding continued with Dorcas and Experience appearing to have the stronger hands. Temperence had an early bid indicating opening point count in her hand, but she quickly dropped out of the bidding.

As a bridge player myself, I enjoyed watching the ladies interact as the game progressed. My wife and I learned how to play while stationed in Japan for three years, as a way to make friends with our neighbors and coworkers. We often got together for an afternoon or evening of bridge, and it proved to be a great way to nurture new friendships.

I've always felt that bridge was a serious game requiring thought and tactics to win … but, what I really enjoyed were the exciting moments when as a defensive player I was able to trump our opponent's winning trick of high cards. Those moments were worth enduring all the more mundane hands that became routine after a while. These were moments when the winners … unsuspecting and confident … suddenly became the losers as their strategy of play fell apart.

Temperence was of like temperament, and she often underbid her hand in order to create such situations. The game I was watching on this day seemed to be heading in that direction.

Once bidding concluded, Dorcas and Experience won the bid at 4 spades … Dorcas, as declarer, was to play the game and Experience laid down her cards and became the dummy. Mary, at Dorcas' left, led the first card and play began … as did their chatter.

"Well, Mary," said Dorcas as she scooped up the first trick. "It looks like we're off to a good start. Only nine more tricks and the first game is ours. By the way, Temperence, what's the latest gossip from the rowdy folks down at the tavern?"

"You should know," Temperence replied. "They're still talking about that fracas you caused when you stopped by and gloated about your husband's rise to town clerk. They seemed to have doubts about the fairness of his testimony as town surveyor in several important real estate cases."

"Oh, I don't seem to recall whatever you're referring to," responded Dorcas, laughing. "Richard and I were always extremely fair and giving of our time to town matters. But, in any case, that paled next to all the shenanigans found in this day's political world. At least our communities were not suffering from a pandemic and social unrest that plague the country today."

They all nodded … and then Experience remarked, "You're right. We have become the best of friends, but we lived in simpler times. However, our memories are of the challenges that caused us to cope and grow as a country. We didn't always get it right, but our efforts on the frontiers of what was to become the greatest nation in the world helped move us along the right path. We all should be commended for putting in place the foundations for this democracy."

"True … true," agreed Dorcas. "But now, back to our game. It's my fourth lead and I'm about to start a run that will win my four spade game." She led the queen of hearts to the ace-jack in the dummy. "Well, Mary ... do you have the king?"

Mary grimaced, and sadly laid her king of hearts on the trick to force dummy to play the ace. "You may win this trick, Dorcas, but don't count your chickens yet."

Dorcas smiled confidently and pulled the ace from the dummy, thinking it would win the trick, but Temperence slowly sat back and said, "Mary, you are so right. When is an ace not dominant? The answer ... when a lowly trump can be played to override the three high cards on the table." And, with a flourish, she plopped the two of spades on the ace, king, and queen of hearts to take the trick.

Dorcas and Experience both flopped back in their chairs as surprise and anxiety crossed their faces. "Well, I didn't see that coming," said Dorcas. Then she watched as Temperence grinned and took the next four tricks ... setting the bidders who cruised to a loss by two tricks. This scenario was repeated several more times during my viewing of their play, with trumps seemingly popping up at the most opportune times to win the hand.

At the end of their get-together as the cards were put back into their boxes, Temperence couldn't stop grinning as she said, "Trumps definitely ruled this day, but I fervently hope the good fortune trump brought to this game continues for us in the future." Dorcas and Experience grumbled.

Then, suddenly, all four ladies rose from the table and turned in my direction. They were smiling and Dorcas, speaking for the foursome, said, "You are here for a reason, Jim, and you must heed what we have to tell you.

"You may think you know how your life will proceed, but like our little bridge game today, it can go in quite different directions. You never know when a trump out there will interrupt and alter life's flow. You must take things in stride and never doubt that the game of life has a mind of its own."

"Yes," continued Experience. "Focus on what you have within your control, and give those matters 100 percent of your abilities and emotion. If we all did that, the future would take care of itself."

Mary carefully added, "But, don't be afraid to stand together with those who share your beliefs, and voice your fully thought-out opinions forcefully when your audience is receptive."

"And by all means," Temperence emphasized, "Enjoy what you have. After all, even in the worst of times, your family and friends are worth the time you share. Just look at us … four ladies from differing times and often 'cheeky' with each other, but we remain best of friends … even in our current ethereal states."

With that, the four apparitions from my family tree faded away.

***

Here's another one of those 101-word tales that I insert here to catch my breath before the next story...

The Cookie

I was ten years old when I first heard the word 'Trump'. My parents were playing a card game called 'bridge', and it seemed a good thing when they said: 'trump'. Their opponents groaned in response.

I used the term sparingly. My only memory of using it was when my mom gave me the last cookie and I told my sister, "My wants trump your wants ... ha, ha!"

I shouldn't have been so arrogant, but brothers will be that way. And then came Donald Trump, and my sense was he wanted the last cookie ... "ha, ha!"

Many people groaned.

***

A Late Addition......

A Man Named Trump

The Beginning

This is a story of politics and intrigue ... success and failure. It explores what impact a political outsider can have on a country's orbit in national and international affairs ... an exciting tale in which all involved have an opinion or two. In fact, the divisiveness engendered is at the heart of my story.

My name is Jim and I will be the narrator of this tumultuous tale. I consider myself a somewhat impartial observer of the turmoil and bitter divides that rocked the nation during our story's duration.

Our main character is a wealthy businessman named Donald Trump, who aspired to become President of the United States of America. After his success in real estate and entertainment, and being disappointed in what he saw as uninspired political leadership, he was convinced he could do better ... and he threw his hat in the ring.

I viewed him as a 'common man', although very rich ... a working man coping with his environment ... sort of like Ralph Kramden and Ed Norton ... with a liberal dose of Don Rickles thrown in to aggravate his opposition. But I also saw a lot of the marketing side of Sam Walton in him ... he brought a business acumen to bear as he directed the 'ship-of-state'.

Others saw him as a buffoon ... a tactless clown without the gravitas needed for true leadership ... a dangerous president who would divide the country and harm international relationships. They did everything possible to disrupt his presidency and cause him political harm ... with a goal to end his reign for the good of the country sooner rather than later.

Most saw him as an outsider who approached the presidency with varying degrees of success.

I must admit, during the primaries leading up to his run in the 2016 election, I was not a fan of Donald Trump. While I thought he brought a freshness to the campaign in terms of 'telling it like it is' and positioning himself as the 'outsider' candidate, I considered him a novice who would easily be defeated by Hillary ... the odds on favored Democratic candidate.

I bounced from favoring one Republican opponent to the next, when each withdrew from the race as Trump gained momentum. It didn't matter how much they spent, the degree of political clout they brought to bear, or how prominent was their name recognition, the 'Donald' rolled right over each in turn.

Trump was everywhere. Television news shows gave him a free platform from which he created news simply by being Donald Trump. The media couldn't get enough of him. He offered an unending stream of interviews and news bites to get his message out, and that enabled him to compete effectively in spite of being outspent nearly two to one.

By the time he was anointed as the Republican candidate he had ruffled so many feathers amongst conservatives that many decided they could not support his candidacy, even though they also despised Hillary. A vocal 'never-Trump' movement was born, and was further aggravated by his promise to eliminate the 'Deep State' … a conspiracy theory which suggested that collusion and cronyism existed within the U.S. government … involving both major parties.

Trump's election was hardly foreordained. All polls, and the media in general, prognosticated that Hillary would win … by wide margins. In spite of my disdain for his personality … maybe because I couldn't see myself giving in to the Democratic platform … I eventually recognized that Trump was endorsing the programs in the general election that I believed in, and I voted for him.

Surprisingly, Donald Trump won the election … and once the Hillary fans dried their tears … the 'fun' began in earnest!

The Trump Presidency

Now, I didn't like it when Bill Clinton won the election in 1992 … a rube in the White House meant the nation was surely headed for troubled times. But, I blamed George Bush for not doing enough to win, and considered Bill Clinton the lawful president of the United States. My mantra at the time was: "All hail the President and hello Hicksville till we can bring back the Shining City on the Hill."

As it turned out, there was much accomplished during the Clinton years that was positive and good for the average Joe … all right, I didn't like everything he did … but there was cooperation with and from conservatives when the good of the country was at play. During the Obama years, however, division and obstruction was intensified on both sides of the political spectrum and the mood of the country began a steady decline.

By the time Trump was sworn in, all semblance of doing what was best for the country by the 'opposition' had vanished. Attacks were unleashed on his administration from all quarters … particularly from every Democratic politician (including anti-Trump conservatives) and 90% of media news outlets and pundits. The 'Shining City' slipped further away.

I could go into all the political turmoil experienced during the Trump presidency, but you probably know it well. It was hard to miss. There were inquiries, charges of presidential lying, biased media, secret meetings, investigations, shady characters, special prosecutors, an impeachment trial ... all designed to minimize Trump's success and remove him from office. And it began even before Trump had won the 2016 election.

In spite of this, Trump led the country to record-setting economic and employment success, installed more favorable global trade treaties, strengthened the constitutional presence on the Supreme Court, strengthened military capability, avoided wars, relaxed tensions in the Middle East and Korean Peninsula, strengthened ties to Israel, and spoke out for more favorable monetary participation in international organizations.

As was true of these or any other positive developments during the Trump years, the liberal media by and large ignored them or minimized their significance. I just wonder what might have been accomplished if politics had been set aside and the good of the nation had been the goal of all parties? And if the media had fairly reported the news, giving credit where due and investigating to insure that transparency of events was maintained? Instead, anger, vindictiveness, bias ... politics in its most corruptive form ...held sway.

Then in 2020, three major disruptions to the country occurred which negatively impacted the

Trump presidency. First, there were wide-spread racial protests, riots and looting stemming from the police killing of George Floyd and other black 'innocents'. There was a push for 'defunding police' which led to increased lawlessness. 'Black Lives Matter' became the rallying cry and, except for his loyal base, Trump was widely lambasted for fueling the civil unrest with his rhetoric and for failing to empathize with the movement.

Second, 2020 was also the year of the Pandemic from China ... the Coronavirus (COVID 19) ... which resulted in widespread infections and deaths ... and drastic political and economic reactions. Fear gripped the nation.

Major efforts were mobilized by the administration to create a vaccine to treat the virus and ramp up the production of supplies needed to identify and treat those infected - respirators, testing kits, face masks, etc. Early shut-downs of travel and immigration from infected areas of China and Europe were implemented.

Preventative measures were also imposed by politicians at every level to stem the spread of infections ... businesses and events were shut down to minimize the risk of transmissions which resulted in widespread unemployment, economic turmoil, business failures ... and a sense of isolation for a large segment of the country. Again, Trump was criticized for not reacting sufficiently to stem the resulting health crisis.

And third, the divisiveness of the 2020 presidential election solidified the nation's already rampant 'opposition at all costs' attitudes. The final tally of votes resulted in Joe Biden being declared the winner, but, as might be expected in our story, the Trump team did not immediately concede … claiming widespread voter fraud.

All together, what started out with a political upset in 2016 and a refusal by some to accept its results ended after four years with a country deep in crisis … over 400,000 reported deaths in the US from COVID 19, personal freedoms in jeopardy, an economy struggling to avoid a recession, greater racial tensions, and a future that looked bleak to many of us.

The Aftereffects

At this point in my story, I put down my pen and decided to forego any further sermonizing on the overall impact of the Trump presidency … and to avoid any prophesizing on the consequences of his time in office. It's enough that I teased you above with my general observations on the Trump years.

Time will reveal the true assessment of 'A Man Named Trump".

***

U to Z is for Part III

of 'The ABCs of an Old Codger Named Jim'

The chapter 'T is for Trump' closes out Part II of my 'ABCs' book. I've written enough for now and I'm sure you need a break from the exciting imagination of this old codger. But ... don't cringe at the thought ... more is planned as I begin thinking about what to regale you with in Part III.

Of course, as I continue imagining story lines for tales of intrigue, humor and pathos, who knows what will happen. Could my next chapter stimulate my imagination so much that it becomes a book of its own? Could my lack of imagination be so frustrating that I fail to develop any stories at all? Alas, I'm afraid you will be subjected to further readings from this old codger as Part III evolves.

At least that's my plan.

***